The Forbidden Orchard

A Novel by

Eliza Morgan Chase

Global East-West (London)

Contents

1
Crossroads of Life

Priya's Demanding Career

Dr. Priya Sharma stood at the entrance of Mumbai's bustling hospital, the familiar scent of antiseptic mingling with the faint aroma of street food wafting through the air. Each day, she traded her bright dreams for the grueling realities of medical practice, diving into a world where compassion met chaos. Her stethoscope hung around her neck like a medal—an emblem of her dedication to healing. Yet today, the weight of expectations pressed heavily on her shoulders. The demands of her job often felt insurmountable, draining her spirit, even as she whispered words of comfort to her patients.

Her compassion radiated through every corridor she traversed, but with each small victory, doubt crept closer. Was this all her life would ever be? Behind the confident facade, a yearning for something more—a deeper connection, a richer experience—flickered like an ember, refusing to be snuffed out. At home, her husband Rohan greeted her with a warm smile and well-prepared meals, yet there was an unspoken distance between them; his kindness lacked the passion she craved. She often wondered if anyone understood the loneliness of carrying such burdens within her heart.

As the clock ticked towards twelve, a familiar wave of exhaustion washed over her, an unsettling reminder of the fine line between compassion and burnout. Dismissing her inner turmoil, Priya focused on her next patient flash of hope in her eyes. But each moment with the patients reminded her of what lay outside these hospital walls—a longing for a life filled with vibrancy and spontaneity. The clock chimed again, this time coldly signaling the irrefutable truth: with each passing day, she edged closer to an ever-growing abyss of unfulfillment, teetering on the edge of something impossibly profound that stayed just out of reach.

Amidst the cacophony of medical jargon and the tapestry of human lives she held in her hands, an unexpected thought began to take root: was it time for her to take control of her own narrative? With an impending medical conference that beckoned from the horizon, excitement mingled with apprehension. Would she find her voice amidst the authority of her colleagues, or would it further imprison her in a life defined by duty? The crossroads loomed before her, the path forward twisted and uncertain. As the chime of the clock resonated in her ears, Priya felt a flicker of courage ignite within her—a challenge she could no longer ignore.

One thought echoed: escape. Escape from the relentless pace, from the weary smile she wore at home, and from the invisible chains that bound her to a life devoid of passion. She found herself staring into the looking glass, contemplating a choice that would define her—opting either for her patient duties or a chance at rekindling the fiery essence of her own existence. The thought thrilled and terrified her in equal measure, and amid this turmoil, she felt a surge of something she hadn't in long—a hope for rediscovery, led by the promise of a new beginning.

Rohan: The Reliable Partner

Rohan always prided himself on being the steady rock in Priya's life. As an engineer, he was methodical and logical, qualities that grounded their relationship in a comfortable routine. They had built a life together that many would envy—shared meals, pleasant conversations, and a deep respect for one another's careers. Yet beneath the surface of their orderly existence lay an undercurrent of unfulfilled desires, especially for Priya.

As Priya rushed through her days in the bustling corridors of the hospital, each life she saved reinforcing her passion for medicine, she felt a growing chasm between her professional triumphs and her personal life. Rohan had always been there, his unwavering support providing her with a sense of security amidst the chaos. But the affection that she craved was often overshadowed by his practicality. She longed for spontaneous gestures, passionate exchanges, but Rohan remained happily anchored to his routine.

While Priya was engulfed in the demands of her career, Rohan often found solace in his hobbies, diving into projects that consumed his evenings. Priya appreciated his dedication; it allowed her time to focus on her patients. However, that reliability, that comfortable companionship that he offered, now felt more like a barrier to her emotional fulfillment. Every interaction between them seemed laced with both familiarity and an invisible distance that she was desperate to bridge. As nights turned into weeks and weeks bled into months, Priya's heart ached for the spice of passion that had been stifled by the predictability of their life together.

One evening, sitting across the dinner table, Priya caught Rohan's gaze as he meticulously cut his food into equal halves. The flicker of something unspoken passed between them, an acknowledgment of the complexities of their intimacy. Yet, she felt the air thicken with the questions she dare not voice. Could she ever articulate her yearning for more, or had she condemned herself to the reliable embrace of a partnership lacking fervor? A storm of emotions roiled within her, intertwining with the prospect of change—a change that seemed to shimmer, tantalizingly just out of reach.

An Unfulfilled Heart

Dr. Priya Sharma stood at the threshold of her bustling life in Mumbai, her thoughts a whirlwind of conflicting emotions. She had become adept at donning the mask of a dedicated physician, a compassionate healer who commanded respect from her colleagues and patience from her patients. Yet, as she tossed her stethoscope into the leather bag, a shadow of discontent loomed large in her heart. The accolades, the late-night shifts, the lives she saved—none of it could fill the aching void that tugged insistently at her soul.

The truth was insidiously simple: beneath her professional façade, Priya felt unfulfilled in her personal life. Rohan, her husband, was a dependable partner, but he was also a reflection of the comfort she had settled for—reliable yet passionless. Their conversations meandered around household duties and mundane responsibilities, devoid of the spark that had once ignited her dreams of a love that could transcend the ordinary. It left her yearning for something more, something deeper, that seemed perpetually out of reach.

The irony stirred bitterness within her. She had carved a niche in an unforgiving medical world, advocating for her patients with empathy and skill, yet felt like an imposter at home, playing a role that was growing increasingly hollow. Could anyone understand her plight? The longing for connection, for heart-thumping excitement, pulsed through her veins like an untamed creature desperately seeking escape. And as she stepped out into the chaos of the Mumbai streets, the sensation only intensified, beckoning her toward uncharted territories of the heart.

With every honking car and bustling pedestrian, the weight of her discontent grew heavier. It was the unfulfilled promise of life whispering, daring her to confront her deepest desires. What if she could find that exhilarating connection she craved? What if she could break free from the invisible chains of expectation that bound her? The thought sent a shiver of exhilaration down her spine, a tantalizing notion of fleeing the confines of her existence to seek out the unknown.

In the swirling atmosphere of longing and fear, Priya remained uncertain of what lay ahead. The echoes of her ambition mingled with her silent screams for passion, and deep within, an unmistakable urge surfaced—an urge to reclaim the narrative of her life. Her heart stirred at the precipice of change, yet the looming specter of duty shackled her spirit, leaving her hovering at the crossroads of decision. She inhaled deeply, readying herself for the tumult that would follow. Change was inevitable, but at what cost? With uncertainty shadowing her every thought, Priya couldn't shake the sensation that the story of her heart was just beginning.

2
Fortress of Tradition

Zayed's Legacy of Wealth

Sheikh Zayed bin Sultan Al-Thani sat in his grand office overlooking the skyline of Doha, a city that seemed to thrive on the expanse of his wealth. Gilded furniture framed the walls, and an intricately woven carpet mapped the floor with patterns of rich tradition. As the charismatic businessman in his late thirties, Zayed had become an emblem of luxury and power, revered within elite circles. Yet today, the weight of expectation pressed down upon him like an unrelenting storm cloud, threatening to overshadow the vibrance of his life.

He glanced at the framed photo on his desk, showing him with Sheikha Fatima and their three children, a portrait of familial bliss intertwined with societal obligation. Underneath this veneer, the truth was more complex; the moments of joy felt superficial when buried beneath the mantle of his duties. It was his legacy, built on the backbone of generations, that often painted a picture of success to the world, but the brushstrokes of his own desires remained unfulfilled.

A knock on the door echoed through the vast expanse of the room, pulling him from his reverie. Fatima, with her polished elegance, entered, her face a mask of concern.

"Zayed, we have guests coming tonight—important ones. Your father expects you to handle the discussions regarding the new business venture with the overseas investors. This is pivotal for our reputation," she stated, her voice steady yet sympathetic.

He nodded, a practiced smile plastered on his face, but inside, the knot of frustration tightened further. The pressure of family expectations loomed large, every gathering a reminder that his worth was measured not just by dedication, but by results.

"Of course, my dear," he replied.

But his heart yearned for something more than polite conversations and the suffocating small talk that accompanied them. He longed for genuine connections, untainted by the obligations of wealth and status.

As the evening approached and guests adorned their finery, Zayed felt like a performer in a grand play, rehearsed actions dictating every interaction. The laughter, the clinking of glasses, the network of political and economic strategists... it all buzzed around him, yet he lingered at the edges, an observer in the grand narrative of his own success.

Where was the passion that once ignited his spirit? He recalled the fleeting moments at the medical conference in Dubai, the unexpected connection with Dr. Priya Sharma that flickered like a candle against the backdrop of his gilded cage. Her intelligence, her compassion—they haunted him. In the sanctuary of his own thoughts, he conjured images of her laughter, the spark of curiosity in her eyes when they discussed their worlds. Could she, too, feel this undeniable tension that electrified the air between them?

Tonight, as he entertained influential investors, he couldn't ignore the gnawing sensation that came with his hidden yearnings. He was a man steeped in tradition, but it was that very tradition that encased him in solitude. Was it possible, he wondered, to forge a path that allowed space for desire, for true connection, amidst the murmurs of propriety?

As the guests moved through the rooms with faux warmth and scripted interactions, he felt the walls closing in. Each smile was a reminder of the choices he had made—the ones that bound him to a life written by someone else's script. He found himself at a crossroads, longing for liberation and grappling with the familiar pull of duty. Would he continue to uphold a legacy built on wealth, forsaking his silent desires, or would he dare to step into the unknown?

The evening wore on, conversations becoming a cacophony, and just as he was about to retreat into the solitude of his thoughts, he caught sight of a familiar figure at the edge of his mind's eye. A woman who flashed into view momentarily, her presence magnetic and undeniable. Could it be? The question ignited a blaze within him. What if she was here? And in that heart-stopping moment, everything he felt about life, family, and legacy spiraled into one striking reality—the choices he faced weren't merely about wealth, but the pursuit of genuine connection, a journey overshadowed by the fortress of tradition he was ensnared within.

Pressure of Family Expectations

Sheikh Zayed bin Sultan Al-Thani stood at the panoramic window of his luxurious office, gazing over the sprawling city of Doha. The skyline shimmered in the golden hues of the setting sun, yet a storm brewed within him. The very privilege that surrounded him—the wealth, the power, the respect—had become a gilded cage. Each day was an intricate ballet of duty and expectation, dictated not by his own desires but by the longstanding traditions of his family.

The weight of his lineage rested heavily upon his shoulders, a legacy stretching back centuries. He held a prominent position in the community, a role that demanded adherence to cultural norms, the preservation of status, and the perpetuation of family honor. Yet, as he reflected on the years of his life spent in service of these ideals, a question gnawed at him: what of his own desires? What of his yearning for a life rich with connection, passion, and genuine love?

His thoughts drifted to Sheikha Fatima, his wife of many years. An intelligent and admirable woman, she embodied the values expected of her, yet their relationship seldom transcended the boundaries of societal expectations. Their marriage, arranged with astute foresight, secured the interests of their families, but left little room for the vulnerable intimacy he craved. As a father, he sought to exemplify the attributes that had been instilled in him, nurturing their three children not only in wealth but in values. Yet, he could sense a growing divide—an echo of the hidden yearnings stirring within him, whispers of a heart longing to break free from the stifling confines of convention.

The clatter of his phone interrupted his reverie. He glanced at the screen and felt a flutter of unease. It was a reminder for the upcoming family meeting, where expectations would again be laid bare under the scrutiny of family elders. Another discussion about future endeavors—another round of sacrifices to appease those who prioritized reputation over individual happiness. He sighed. As much as he admired the ambitions set forth by his family, he felt less like an architect of his life and more like a marionette, strings pulled in a direction he had little say in.

The upcoming meeting weighed on him like a heavy shroud, cloaked in societal expectations that offered no room for dissent. Within the fortress of tradition, where he was perceived as a paragon of success and propriety, he felt utterly trapped. The thought that kept him awake at night was not the legacy he was to inherit but the future that lay before him, one devoid of authentic fulfillment. Would he one day look back at his life and regret the dreams he sacrificed at the altar of tradition? The voices of his ancestors echoed like an unyielding chorus in his mind: family first, honor above all.

Pacing the length of his stately office,

Zayed felt the pulse of anxiety quicken. The clash between responsibility and desire surged within him, escalating into a tempest. As the meeting drew nearer, he could almost feel the walls closing in around him—each brick representing an unyielding expectation, each mortar a binding commitment to shield his family's name. Would he dare disrupt this meticulously crafted existence? Or was he destined to stay within the confines of a life that, though enviable in the eyes of many, was ultimately hollow? The questions spun in his mind like a whirlwind, each one inching him closer to a precipice he could neither ignore nor escape.

With each passing moment, the urgency within him swelled, driven by memories of unfulfilled moments and undiscovered passions. What awaited him on the other side of this impending meeting? Would it be merely another stanza in the poem of familial obligation, or could it become the pivotal point from which he could claim his own narrative? He feared what was to come but sensed that, ultimately, it would lead him down a path no longer obscured by the shadows of expectation.

Hidden Yearnings

Sheikh Zayed bin Sultan Al-Thani gazed out from the expansive balcony of his Doha home, the golden sands stretching towards the horizon. A landscape marked by opulence, where tradition wrapped itself around the present like an intricate tapestry. But even in this magnificent fortress of wealth and lineage, Zayed felt a gnawing void within him, a longing that resonated deeper than the echo of power and influence his name commanded.

Every Sunday, a parade of high-profile meetings ushered in faces adorned with smiles but thick with ulterior motives. Zayed found himself performing a dance he had mastered since childhood, a performance expected of those of his stature. The family expectations weighed heavily on his shoulders, demanding him to uphold a legacy that seemed to strangle his own desires. Behind his calm and charismatic demeanor lay an impulse to break free from the rigid confines of his traditional world.

Yet, there was something unsettling about the comfort his life offered. The plush carpets of his home were soaked in ancestral pride, but they also muffled his cries for authentic connection. His marriage to Sheikha Fatima, grounded in respect and shared responsibilities, left him yearning for a more profound emotional intimacy. As he scrolled through his phone, the vibrant image of Priya surfaced—the doctor he had met at the conference whose presence stirred something within him he had long believed buried. A flicker of hope ignited, mingling with the fear of what such feelings could unravel.

The faint sound of children playing in the distance brought him momentarily back to the present, yet the laughter felt foreign, resonating in stark contrast to the turmoil within. Closing his eyes, he envisioned Priya's laughter; it was like a siren's call, drawing him into an uncharted territory laden with possibility. Could he dare to explore it? Would he sacrifice the life expected of him for a fleeting chance at genuine companionship?

With a heavy heart, Zayed pondered the uncharted path ahead. The weight of his unfulfilled yearnings collided with the societal pressures that tethered him to tradition. The enigmatic pull of Priya, with her unexpressed dreams and haunting beauty, challenged him to reconsider all he had been led to believe. What would he be willing to risk for the promise of something real, authentic, and life-altering?

As dusk began to settle over the city, casting long shadows on the ground, he knew he stood on the precipice of a decision that could redefine his destiny. The boundaries of duty and desire loomed before him, and each heartbeat whispered the same challenge: to leap into the unknown or to retreat into the safety of the familiar. Yet, deep down, in that hidden chamber of his heart where true yearning resided, he felt an exhilarating sense of fear mixed with longing—an undeniable beckoning to confront the most profound questions of his life.

3

The Pulse of Progress

The Medical Conference Intentions

As Dr. Priya Sharma stood in front of the mirror, adjusting her crisp white coat, she felt a familiar jolt of anticipation. The upcoming medical conference promised a platform to present her groundbreaking research on cardiac care, a subject she was both passionate about and proficient in. It felt like a culmination of years of hard work, but beneath that excitement lurked a sense of dread. What would attending this high-profile event mean for her professional reputation—and, more disturbingly, her personal life?

Every detail mattered, from the meticulously crafted slides to the sharpness of her thoughts during the presentation. Yet, her mind often wandered to thoughts of Zayed, the enigmatic businessman she'd seen at the conference's preliminary meetings. He was not just a participant; he represented an entirely different world, teeming with experiences that seemed so far removed from her own. Priya recalled the briefest of interactions with him and how those few moments left a palpable tension in the air. She couldn't deny it—something intrigued her about him that stirred feelings she had suppressed for too long.

As she made her way through the bustling corridors of the convention center, the atmosphere buzzed with a palpable energy of intellect and innovation. Doctors and researchers mingled, exchanging insights and the occasional smile, each more dynamic and accomplished than the last. Priya wondered, amid this sea of brilliance, whether her voice would resonate, whether she would matter here. But more than that, she thought of the cultural chasms she had yet to navigate, the conversations that would challenge her notions and, perhaps, lead her to unexpected intersections.

Her contemplation was abruptly interrupted by the sound of an announcement echoing through the hall. It was time for her session. As she stepped into the auditorium, heart racing, every eye turned toward her, a thousand expectations weighing upon her. Her palms felt clammy, but she steadied her mind, recalling the importance of her message. Yet, as she began to speak, a passing glance caught her—Zayed in the audience, his presence a mesmerizing anchor amid the sea of unfamiliar faces. Their eyes met, and the world around them faded. In that singular moment, she felt the stirrings of a connection that could unravel everything.

After the presentation, she felt a rush of accomplishment, tempered by the awareness of Zayed's gaze from across the room. When the session ended, a mix of applause and chatter filled the space, but the weight of his presence lingered like a tempest ready to unfold. Would she simply let this sensation fade, or could she explore this intricate web of emotions that was beginning to weave itself into her reality? The choices lay heavy upon her shoulders, and each subsequent moment felt like a countdown to an inevitable confrontation where her heart's true intentions would collide with her bound commitments. The tension vibrated in the air like an unplayed note, each passing second amplifying the stakes of her desires.

Unpacking Cultural Differences

As Priya stood at the polished edge of the conference hall in Dubai, her heart raced with an anticipation that felt almost foreign to her. The brilliant lights above cast a warm glow, illuminating the diverse tapestry of medical professionals gathered from across the globe. She had always thrived in the clinical environment of Mumbai, where every decision weighed heavily with consequences and humanity intertwined with science. But here, amid the many languages and cultures, she felt a wave of insecurity wash over her—one that stemmed from the vast differences that separated her world from those of her international peers.

She found herself thinking about the subtle nuances of communication, not merely in speech but in gestures and expressions. Would her colleagues be receptive to the Indian form of hierarchy, where respect was deeply rooted in culture? Would they understand her tendency to blend personal warmth with professionalism? As she made her way through the crowd, she couldn't shake the feeling of being a stranger in a land bursting with modernity and liberated norms—an alien among visionaries forging paths she could scarcely imagine.

Then there was the echo of laughter, the spontaneous camaraderie that seemed to flow effortlessly between the delegates. In contrast, she felt restrained by expectations—both her own and those of her culture. Her meticulous notes felt heavier now, laden with the weight of her intentions, the desire to make an impact but hindered by fears of missteps. Priya's thoughts drifted back to Rohan, the comfort of her marriage that both anchored her and chained her to a life of predictability. She wrestled with the thought of how culture shaped relationships, how the people around her thrived in an open dialogue that felt intimidating yet invigorating.

With each passing moment, the assembly buzzed with energy, the shared commitment to health and progress uniting them in their pursuit of understanding and healing. Yet, within her, the strain of contrasting traditions—a clash of expectations—danced provocatively. It was in this charged atmosphere that she caught sight of Zayed, his presence cutting through the rhetoric of the crowd like a beacon. He exuded an effortless charm, grounded by his own cultural intricacies, navigating the fine line of tradition and modernity that echoed her own struggles. As their eyes met across the room, a realization washed over her; the barriers of their backgrounds could simultaneously enrich and complicate their interaction.

The unfolding minutes felt excruciatingly slow, her mind racing as she traced the contours of their respective lives through mere observations. Instead of engaging in small talk like everyone else, would they find a shared language that transcended the barriers of their worlds? As cultural curiosities collided, she could not shake the feeling that behind every polite smile lie deeper uncertainties. And with the conference presenting opportunities for open dialogue, could they expose their vulnerabilities and connect on a level beyond mere professional aspirations? The questions loomed like shadows, growing longer with the ticking clock.

As Priya moved closer to the group, she felt the weight of unspoken words suffocating her excitement, churning within her like a distant storm. It was the allure of new connections and untrodden paths that pumped the pulse of progress into her veins, yet the reality of cultural expectations cast an ever-deepening shadow over her heart. With Zayed's gaze lingering on her, a whisper of hope dared to spark amidst a storm of doubt, igniting a fire that would challenge everything she thought she knew about love, duty, and crossing borders.

First Impressions of Dubai

The moment Dr. Priya Sharma stepped off the plane, the air buzzed with an electric vibrancy that felt achingly foreign yet intoxicatingly inviting. Dubai, a gleaming oasis amidst the arid desert, exuded an undeniable charm, a spectacle designed to dazzle. While her hometown of Mumbai hummed with an organized chaos, Dubai presented itself as a masterstroke of precision—a seamless blend of modernity and tradition, glistening structures rising with ambition and purpose.

As she made her way through the airport, Priya couldn't help but gaze upward at the soaring ceilings adorned with opulent chandeliers that shimmered like stars in a twilight sky. The aroma of rich Arabic coffee wafted through the air, merging with the scent of exquisite perfumes. It was a far cry from the monsoon-soaked streets of Mumbai; the contrast was stark yet exhilarating, an awakening to a world brimming with possibilities.

Dressed in her tailored conference attire, she felt a mixture of excitement and trepidation. The city felt alive, pulsating with ambition, and somewhere within that vast urban sprawl lay a promise of opportunity—voices yet to be heard, innovations waiting to unfurl. She was here to present her research, yet all she could think of was the intricate tapestry of lives interwoven into the fabric of this city that seemed to embrace her with open arms.

As she approached her hotel, her heart raced at the sight of the Burj Khalifa soaring majestically above the skyline. It was more than just a building; it was a monument to human aspiration, an architectural marvel that proclaimed to the world the prowess of innovation and determination. Priya found herself yearning to touch that soaring pinnacle, to share in the ambition that propelled it to reach the heavens.

Overwhelmed by the grandeur surrounding her, she took a moment to compose herself in the lavish lobby suffused with golden tones and luxurious decor. Yet amid the glamour, a sliver of uncertainty crept into her thoughts. Would she truly fit into this world, one so different from her own? As she stood there, a flicker of self-doubt whispered, threatening to overshadow her excitement. Her memories of the bustling streets of Mumbai faded into the background, and she felt the weight of expectations pressing against her—her own and those of the attendees, many of whom she believed were seasoned professionals, perhaps even pioneers in their fields.

But even as doubt lingered, another emotion sparked within her—a burning desire to make her mark, to prove her worth and showcase her work on this international stage. The unfamiliar challenges and cultural nuances felt palatable, the thrill of the unknown beckoning her like a siren. Priya breathed deeply, allowing the warm air of possibility to invigorate her as she stepped forward with renewed resolve, ready to delve into the heart of Dubai, where aspirations ran wild.

As the conference commenced the next day, Priya's anticipation swelled. She felt like a mere piece in a grand mosaic, each attendee a vibrant hue. Among the sea of delegates, her eyes flickered from one distinguished figure to another. It was only when she spotted a tall, distinguished man speaking to a group—his presence commanding yet approachable—that she felt an inexplicable pull. Sheikh Zayed bin Sultan Al-Thani, his name echoed in whispers around her as the conference buzzed to life, each word steeped in respect. Little did she know, their paths would entwine in ways that would shake the very foundations of her understanding of love, duty, and passion.

As she made her way toward the stage for her presentation, the essence of Dubai felt like a tantalizing tease, both exhilarating and foreboding. What would the future hold in this city fueled by dreams? Priya's heart raced not only from her impending presentation but from the potential for something extraordinary to unfurl—a ripple that might change everything she believed possible.

4
Fate's Intrusion

The Accidental Encounter

As Priya navigated the crowded hall of the conference center, the low hum of voices and the clicking of heels blended into a soundscape she had grown accustomed to. Each step forward was fueled by ambition and purpose; she was here to present her research, to advocate for the patients who depended on her. Yet, amidst the throng of medical professionals, a lingering sense of isolation trailed her like a shadow.

Meanwhile, Sheikh Zayed observed the lively atmosphere with a practiced calm, the weight of family expectations hanging heavily on his shoulders, much like the opulent wristwatch that adorned his wrist. The conference was a world where he could momentarily escape the constraints of his privileged life, but even here, fleeting connections proved elusive. As he turned to scan the sea of faces, something—no, someone—caught his eye.

In an instant, the world faded around him. Priya, with her dark hair cascading in soft waves, was engaged in conversation, her animated gestures bringing life to her words. He couldn't help but notice the fire in her eyes—an intensity he longed to share but had not found in his curated existence. The pang of curiosity surged within him, a desire to bridge the distance that traditional roles had erected between them.

As Priya turned, her elbow grazed against Zayed's shoulder, a minor bump in the bustling crowd, but their eyes met in that split second—an electric jolt crackled between them. The unspoken words lingered in the space where they stood. Time stretched, and the cacophony of the conference faded into a muted background, allowing only the soft sound of their breaths to reach their ears.

The moment was fleeting, but it ignited something deep within both of them. Priya blinked, catching herself as she hesitated, a strange blend of surprise and intrigue coloring her cheeks. Zayed found himself struck by the warmth of her gaze, a tantalizing promise of an understanding he had all but given up on finding. A silent pact formed in the wake of that accidental meeting, weaving a thread that beckoned them to draw closer, to explore the paths that converged for just a heartbeat in the chaos of the conference.

As they drifted apart into the throng of attendees, an unacknowledged yearning simmered beneath the surface. Priya's heart raced with unwelcome excitement, while Zayed wrestled with the repercussions of their unexpected connection. With each passing moment, that connective spark transformed into something more complex—a curiosity that begged to be explored. Both felt an innate apprehension about the implications of their lives colliding in such an unexpected manner, yet the allure of delving deeper into this newfound connection was impossible to ignore.

As Priya resumed her path to the speaker's podium, she cast a glance over her shoulder, her heart wavering at the thought of Zayed's intense stare still lingering on her. Zayed, in turn, felt the subtle tension pressing against his chest, a reminder of the life he was expected to maintain while secretly hoping for something more—something real amidst the facade of societal expectations. What was meant to be a simple conference had become a doorway into the unexplored territories of their souls, leaving them both breathless and yearning for a glimpse beyond their present realities.

Shared Air of Curiosity

The accidental encounter at the crowded conference hall lingered in the air like the sweet scent of jasmine, subtly intoxicating as Priya bumped into Sheikh Zayed. As their eyes briefly met, an electric charge flickered between them—a lightning bolt of recognition amidst the throngs of attendees, each absorbed in their own pursuits.

Priya felt a ripple of curiosity awaken within her, stirring her from the mechanical rhythm of her life. In that fleeting moment, she saw not just a wealthy businessman but a kindred spirit cloaked in layers of duty and expectation. Zayed's poised demeanor belied an intriguing depth, a soul yearning for something more than the glittering façade of his privileged existence. She wondered: What secrets did he hide behind that charming smile?

As the conference wore on, Priya found herself stealing glances at Zayed, watching him engage effortlessly with other delegates. His laughter took flight, filling the space around him with warmth—a stark contrast to the chilly veneer of her own life back in Mumbai. In those brief moments when their eyes met again, an unspoken question flickered alive: Could they escape the confines of their structured lives and explore what lay beyond the surface?

The weight of their unbidden intrigue settled heavily upon them, a shared air thick with the possibilities of what could be. Each glance felt like a promise, a woven tapestry of affection and uncertainty slowly unfurling under the vast Dubai skyline. Priya's heart raced, caught between the thrill of this unexpected connection and the suffocating ties of her marriage to Rohan.

Then came the decisive moment—Zayed turned slightly, catching Priya mid-stare. Their gazes locked in a silent acknowledgment, heartbeats matching the pulse of the bustling crowd around them. She blinked, a flutter of vulnerability coursing through her as the reality of their respective com-mitments crashed in like a wave against the shore of their newfound curiosity.

As Zayed approached her, the buzz of the conference faded into a distant hum, and everything else seemed to blur. In his deep, rich voice, he asked about her work, each word laden with a gravity that hinted at the depths of his own yearning. It was a simple conversation, yet the implications felt pro-found, resonating within the shared silence created by their growing attraction.

Yet, as they exchanged pleasantries, a shadow of doubt flitted across Priya's mind. What fate would befall them if they allowed this curiosity to bloom beyond the confines of circumstance? Would the risk of stepping into the unknown become a bittersweet revelation or unleash turmoil they were un-prepared to face? The question hung in the air, unasked yet lingering, echoing the deeper complexities of their lives.

With the conference nearing its end and their time growing short, the fraying threads of their respective obligations threatened to pull them apart. Priya could feel the weight of expectation settling upon her shoulders, the compelling need to either turn away from this connection or embrace the faint glimmer of hope it offered. Would they dare to seek solace in this shared air of curiosity, or would they shrink back into the shadows of convention, leaving the mystery unfinished and unfulfilled?

Fleeting Glances

As Priya made her way through the bustling conference hall, the ambient chatter blended with the soft murmur of conversations around her, creating a symphony of professional fervor. She adjusted her glasses, her heart racing not just from the anticipation of her presentation but from a lingering sense of curiosity that she could not quite place. Despite her focus on the task at hand, there was an invisible thread of tension that pulled her thoughts towards a recent encounter, one that had unraveled with unexpected swiftness.

It had been only moments before when she collided with Zayed, quite literally. The accidental meeting ignited something within her, a flicker of interest so striking that it momentarily eclipsed her professional concerns. Their eyes met briefly, connecting in that crowded space, sending a jolt of awareness coursing through her. Was it possible that a mere look could cast aside years of tradition and expectations? Priya shook off the thought, grounding herself in her reality as she adjusted her hair and rehearsed her notes once more.

Yet, the memory of his gaze lingered like a perfume in the air, intoxicating and both exhilarating and frightening. She found her thoughts drifting back to that moment: the way Zayed's rich brown eyes had held hers, a silent question tethered in the space between them. Was he as intrigued by her as she was by him? Shaking her head slightly, Priya moved closer to the podium, her resolve returning, but the fleeting glances exchanged earlier danced like butterflies in her stomach, each beat of her heart pushing the boundaries of her carefully contained world.

Before she could gather her thoughts, she caught sight of Zayed across the hall. He was engrossed in conversation, but even from a distance, she could sense the energy that radiated from him—a charisma that drew people in. For a brief second, their eyes locked again, and time seemed to implode, the chaos of the conference fading into a near silence. Priya's breath hitched as the world around them blurred; it was just the two of them in an unexpected reunion of souls searching for more.

But troubling questions loomed as the moment fractured. What did this mean? The lives they had built, the commitments they had made, loomed like shadows on the periphery of their newfound connection. She felt the weight of her own life, the expectations of a passionless marriage with Rohan pressing heavily against her chest. That moment, those fleeting glances, were both a dangerous crack in her disillusionment and an invitation into a world where desire beckoned like the sun breaking through dark clouds.

As she prepared to step into the spotlight, the tension built, almost suffocating in its intensity. Could she seize this moment, or would she retreat into the safety of her familiar, though unfulfilling, existence? The question hung in the air like an unspoken promise, igniting her heart with uncharted anticipation.

5
Echoes of Curiosity

Subtle Connections Post-Encounter

The conference buzzed around Dr. Priya Sharma as she wandered through the elegantly decorated hallways of the Dubai venue, her mind a whirlpool of thoughts. The brief encounter with Sheikh Zayed bin Sultan Al-Thani lingered in her consciousness, an invisible thread pulling at her heart. It was a chance meeting, a accidental collision of lives that resonated deeper than she had imagined. Each time she recalled their brief exchange, a warmth swelled inside her, not unlike the first rays of the morning sun breaking through the haze of dawn.

Priya found herself thinking of Zayed during her quiet moments, his charm exuding a magnetic allure that overshadowed the familiar confines of her daily life. The contrast of their worlds weighed heavily on her; him, an influential businessman from Qatar, and her, a devoted doctor in bustling Mumbai.

Yet, in that moment, standing in the crowded hall of the conference, their lives had intersected, if only briefly, stirring a curiosity that refused to dissipate. She was drawn to his enigmatic presence, the subtle confidence he carried, and the fleeting glances they exchanged that hinted at uncharted territory.

As the day wore on, Priya's thoughts drifted, entangled in unspoken possibilities. Secrets and duties tethered her to her life in India, to Rohan, whose reliable yet unexciting companionship felt increasingly insufficient. Zayed represented an excitement that ignited a fire within her that she had long suppressed. Yet guilt nagged at the edges of her consciousness like a persistent shadow, reminding her of her commitments and the life she had built. Could she dare to entertain the notion that destiny had woven a new tapestry for her—one that included the enigmatic sheikh? The deeper she delved into her thoughts, the more pronounced the tension within her became, mirroring the pulse of the city outside.

With each passing hour, the fleeting moments with Zayed replayed in her mind like a melody she couldn't shake off. There was a shared air of curiosity, an unexperienced spark igniting something profound, and it left an indelible mark that she couldn't simply erase. Throughout the conference, as she engaged with her peers and presented her research with professionalism, Priya felt an undercurrent of longing that pulled her thoughts back to the shadowy corners of her heart. What if this was more than just a moment? What if it was the echo of something larger, waiting to unfold? A swirl of conflicting emotions threatened to transcend her carefully curated existence, leaving her both exhilarated and terrified.

As the night fell over Dubai, whispers of the day lingered in the air, igniting a yearning within Priya that brewed quietly but insistently. She felt an unrelenting desire to reach out to him, to understand the depths of his world beyond his title and wealth.

The thought ignited the explosive potential of what could be, and in the depth of her solitude, the question loomed larger. How long could she cling to the illusion of her present before the enticing prospect of the unknown beckoned her to leap into the chasm of the forbidden? In her intricate dance of curiosity and longing, outcomes began to unravel silently, promising that the real story was only just beginning.

Reflections on Cultural Differences

As the sun dipped below the horizon, casting a golden hue across the Dubai skyline, Priya stood on her hotel balcony, her heart still racing from the unexpected encounter with Sheikh Zayed. The city pulsated with life below her, an exhilarating blend of ancient tradition and futuristic ambition. She thought of her life in Mumbai, a whirlwind of patient calls and deadlines, where every decision felt laced with the expectations of her family and the weight of her arranged marriage to Rohan. How could two worlds so vastly different forge a connection so profound?

In the quiet of her room, she recalled the way Zayed's eyes sparkled with intelligence, and how his laughter seemed to dismantle the guarded walls she had fortified over the years. There was a certain depth in his understanding of the human experience—a shared sense of longing that transcended their cultural boundaries. While she had returned to a life of solid routines and predictable outcomes, Zayed was encased in his own fortress, burdened by the traditions of a lineage steeped in wealth and expectations.

She pondered the Islamic tradition, the societal expectations that held Sheikh Zayed in a delicate balance of duty towards his family and desire for personal fulfillment. The contrast was staggering. In India, her own struggle involved the balance between professional ambition and the duties as a wife, roles crafted by her family yet felt stifling. Were their differences insurmountable? Or could they uncover common ground in their shared quest for personal authenticity?

Just as she found herself lost in contemplation, a ping from her phone pulled her back to the present. It was a message from Zayed:

> Thinking of our conversation. I believe there's more our worlds can learn from each other.

Her breath hitched. Each word hammered against her sense of propriety, igniting a flame of curiosity amidst the trepidation of stepping beyond the confines of cultural restrictions.

She felt a wave of gratitude rush over her; this dialogue might lead to deeper explorations of empathy and understanding, yet it could also drown her in a sea of conflict. How could she keep her heart locked away when every message tugged at her yearnings? The fabric of their cultures was interwoven with consequences, and the very act of imagining a life shared would force her to confront the impending storm of suspicion that awaited her back in India.

As the lights of Dubai twinkled like stars filled with promise, she feared what revelations could tumble out, much like the escalating pace of her heartbeat. Rohan, her reliable yet uninspiring companion, and Sheikha Fatima, Zayed's dutiful wife, both awaited undisrupted lives, unaware of the undercurrents shifting in the shadows. For now, Priya clung to the thought that perhaps love, though complicated and contentious, could blossom in atmospheres enriched by diversity. But at what cost, she fretted? In a moment of defiance against the grip of her tradition, she typed back:

> And perhaps there's some understanding we could cultivate together.

But as she hit send, a shiver ran down her spine. What would it mean to cross that final boundary? There was no retreat from this connection, the embrace of which set forth an uncertain and dangerous path. The interplay of duty and desire hung precariously in the air, and as the illusion of safety started to crumble, Priya couldn't help but ponder whether she was reaching for a beautiful mirage—one that could either offer solace or strip bare the very fabric of her existence.

Lingering Thoughts

As the days passed after their brief yet impactful encounter, both Priya and Zayed found themselves ensnared in a web of thoughts, endlessly replaying the moment they had shared. Priya sat in her small apartment in Mumbai, surrounded by medical textbooks and the persistent hum of city life, yet her mind was far from the world of diagnoses and patients. Every fleeting moment spent in Zayed's presence lingered like a soft melody, threading its way through her daily routines, leaving a lingering sense of longing. What she had felt in that heart-stopping moment at the conference was more than just curiosity; it was a call to explore a realm she had never dared to venture into.

Meanwhile, in the luxurious surroundings of his office in Doha, Zayed wrestled with his own tumultuous emotions. The polished marble and golden accents of his world felt suffocating as thoughts of Priya danced through his mind like shadows. The weight of his responsibilities to his family and country pressed heavily upon him, yet the image of Priya's genuine smile eclipsed everything else. Had their connection been mere chance, or was it something more profound? He wished to reach out to her, to grasp the threads of fate that had intertwined their paths, but the fear of crossing boundaries held him back, solidifying the walls he was so accustomed to.

Both of them found solace in their respective isolations, yet the distance deepened their yearning. Late at night, Priya would look out of her window at the city's lights twinkling like stars, thoughts of Zayed weaving in and out of her mind. Each passing car below was just a reminder of how fast life moved, yet her own heart had come to a standstill since meeting him.

In Doha, Zayed stared at the horizon, the sun setting over the skyline, casting a warm glow that reminded him of Priya's captivating presence, a vivid reminder of the life he craved but couldn't have. Their hearts beat in synchrony despite the miles that separated them, every pulse echoing a desire unspoken and thought unfulfilled.

And then there came an unavoidable realization that struck them both at the same time: This was no simple infatuation. Both harbored secrets, unspoken feelings that stirred like a tempest within, waiting for the right moment to surge forth. The reality of their lives, their commitments, hung like a pendulum, swinging between duty and desire. In this precarious dance, the question loomed larger than life: How long could they ignore these lingering thoughts before they became something that would shatter the worlds they lived in? As each day passed, the silence became louder, a clamor of unuttered words and unrealized hopes, and Priya and Zayed each felt the weight of inevitability pressing against their hearts, urging them toward an uncertain future.

6

A Helping Hand Across Borders

Reconnecting at the Conference

As the sun dipped below the gleaming skyline of Dubai, cast in warm hues of orange and pink, Priya felt a mix of anticipation and trepidation. The medical conference that had initially seemed like just another professional obligation now shimmered with the potential for connection—an echo of something that had begun with a mere accidental encounter. With each step through the grand hall, she recalled the fleeting yet profound moment shared with Zayed, the enigmatic businessman from Qatar whose presence had stirred emotions deep within her.

When she spotted him across the room, standing confidently beside a display of innovative health technologies, her heart fluttered as if offering a silent salute to the memories they had created, however brief. He turned, his gaze locking with hers, and in that instant, the crowded room faded into a backdrop of murmur and laughter, leaving only the two of them suspended in a shared world of unspoken understanding. Zayed's smile held a warmth that contrasted sharply with the cool professionalism that had defined her interactions all day.

As they approached each other, the barriers of their reality—their spouses, their responsibilities, the expectations of their cultures—seemed to dissolve under the intensity of the moment.

"Dr. Sharma," he said, his voice lower and more inviting than she remembered. "I was hoping for a chance to speak with you again."

It was an invitation shrouded in layers of meaning. They talked about their respective presentations, sharing insights and hopes for progress in their fields, but it was clear that beneath the surface, the original spark had reignited. Priya's pulse quickened, every word exchanged creating a rhythm that echoed with possibilities.

Time slipped as they delved deeper into

their discussion, each moment layering over the last in a slow construction of trust and mutual admiration. Zayed shared tales of his philanthropic efforts, vulnerable threads woven through with the golden fabric of his charm. Priya allowed herself to lean into this dialogue, her professional armor slipping away. The connection unfurled like blossoms under the sun, a mesmerizing dance of minds and hearts, each laugh and shared glance threading them closer together.

But just as the air thickened with simmering potential, a shadow flickered at the edges of her consciousness—a ripple of anxiety that clouded her thoughts. What were they doing? What would the cost be for indulging this compelling connection in a world where they were already tethered to lives filled with obligations? The moment of shared laughter turned into an unspoken dilemma, and Priya fought to hide the turmoil bubbling within.

Before the night could stretch into something more, Zayed's phone buzzed insistently in his pocket, a sound that seemed to resonate with their clandestine reality. His expression shifted, and she noticed the flicker of responsibility crossing his features like a shadow passing before the sun. He glanced toward the door, where the conference's social event would soon begin—an event filled with the very people who would serve as their respective audiences, their families and acquaintances.

Pain lanced through her chest at the thought of them returning to their lives after skirting the edges of something profound. Each of them carried burdens too heavy to set down, yet the bond they were forging felt like an escape they hadn't dared to imagine.

"Priya," he said, concern etching lines on his forehead. "We need to talk. There's so much more I want to say."

His eyes spoke volumes, filled with a mix of longing and fear.

Before she could respond, the atmosphere shifted again, palpable nervous energy igniting the air. Fellow conference attendees began entering, laughter and chatter encroaching on their moment. Reality reasserted itself, powerful and unyielding, forcing them to recognize the brewing storm outside—the expectations, the duties they could not ignore. An invisible thread pulled them apart, tugging at their hearts even as their souls danced in the warmth of possibility.

Their laughter faded, replaced by a tense silence. Standing mere inches apart, they could feel the gravitational pull of longing—the desire to break through the confines of their constructed lives and embrace this raw, untamed connection. With a shared understanding, they stepped back to align themselves once more with the personas they were expected to portray, all while their hearts remained on the precipice of an uncharted emotional precipice. The moment wasn't lost, but in the growing clamor of voices, the future suddenly felt precariously uncertain.

Exploring the Shared Vision

Amidst the sleek modernity of the conference hall in Dubai, Priya and Zayed found themselves enveloped in an atmosphere charged with ambition and purpose. Their previous encounter, marked by an accidental brush of shoulders and fleeting glances, had ignited a spark of curiosity that neither could afford to ignore. As they navigated the sea of attendees, the world around them faded into a muted background, leaving only the connection they shared in stark relief.

"We should collaborate on a session," Zayed suggested, his voice smooth as silk.

Priya felt a flutter of excitement at the prospect. This was not merely a professional overture; it was an invitation to explore the shared vision that had begun to blossom between them, eons away from their daily lives weighed down by duty and expectation.

"Your insights on healthcare disparities in India could align beautifully with our upcoming initiatives," he continued, his eyes steady, revealing a depth of interest that she hadn't anticipated.

Priya's heart raced as she considered the implications. A chance to merge her vision with that of the philanthropic endeavors she had always admired from afar.

"I'd love that," she replied, masking the tremor in her voice with a smile.

Yet, beneath that smile, a storm brewed. Could this potential collaboration turn from a professional alliance into something far more precarious? The weight of their unspoken attraction cast an ever-expanding shadow over her thoughts, reminding her that she stood at the brink of something utterly forbidden.

As they delved into animated discussions about their aspirations, exploring not just medical advancements but also deeper societal impacts, the lines of professionalism began to blur. This wasn't just a sharing of ideas; it felt like a merging of paths, fates intertwined by a profound understanding of each other's struggles. Zayed spoke passionately about his foundation's goals — improving lives while upholding integrity in an ever-complicated world. Priya found herself hanging onto every word, captivated not only by his intellect but by the vulnerability lacing his aspirations.

Yet, amidst the exhilaration of new ideas and the budding connection, an insistent voice nagged at the back of her mind. What did this mean for them? What if their families discovered this collaboration — this connection — turning what felt like magnetic attraction into societal scandal? The complications of their respective worlds weighed heavily upon her shoulders, threatening to pull her back into the constraints of reality.

In a moment of silence, they found themselves gazing out over the bustling conference floor, the lives of others moving rapidly while they stood still. It was in that hushed moment that Zayed turned to her, his expression a blend of earnestness and vulnerability.

"Priya, do you believe people like us can truly shift the narrative?" he asked, eyes searching hers with an intensity that sent a thrill down her spine.

She felt the enormity of his question and the implications rattling within her own heart. Would they truly become catalysts for change, or would their growing connection only serve to deepen the chasm between duty and desire?

Before she could answer, a loud commotion erupted from a nearby panel discussion, drawing their attention away from each other and back to the thrumming reality that surrounded them. Yet, within that distraction, the unspoken tension was explosive. Bound by their responsibilities but yearning for more, they existed on the edge of a precipice — where mere collaboration might transform into an emotional entanglement neither was prepared to navigate.

As the noise swirled around them, a silent agreement settled between them — they would explore this shared vision, no matter where it might lead. But little did they know, stepping into this uncharted territory would test their resolve and complicate their lives in ways they could never foresee.

Building Professional Respect

As the conference progressed, Priya found herself increasingly drawn to Zayed. Their interactions, though laced with professionalism, hinted at something deeper. The way he addressed her ideas with genuine interest, nodding thoughtfully whenever she spoke, made her feel seen in a world often overshadowed by her achievements. It was a refreshing change from the conversations that often surrounded her in Mumbai, where her passion sometimes seemed to blend into the ambient noise of routine and obligation.

During a breakout session focused on health initiatives, Zayed approached her, his expression earnest.

"I believe your research on maternal health could greatly benefit our foundation's work," he said, his voice smooth yet tinged with fervor.

Suddenly, the weight of their cultural

differences melted away, replaced by an undeniable connection rooted in shared values and aspirations. They brainstormed how to implement Priya's strategies in Qatar, their eyes lighting up with enthusiasm, transforming a simple professional exchange into a budding partnership.

As they interacted, an invisible thread began weaving their professional lives together. Zayed's insights were profound, grounding Priya's lofty dreams with the realities of implementation. The respect she felt for him grew; he was not just a businessman but a man burdened by legacy yet driven by a desire for meaningful change. Each meeting, while seemingly tied to their careers, amplified the tension simmering beneath the surface—a steely connection that teetered on the precipice of something uncharted.

But as the conference moved toward its climax, Priya knew the stakes had risen. Each moment spent in his company was a reminder of the emotional bond deepening alongside their professional rapport. They laughed over shared stories of cultural misunderstandings, but the laughter echoed in the back of her mind—was it worth the risk? The lines between respect and something more began to blur, leading to late-night conversations where their revelations felt both thrilling and dangerous.

And then, on the final night of the conference, as they stood under the glittering lights of Dubai's skyline, their futures stretching before them, Zayed made a bold suggestion.

"What if we collaborated further? I'd like to see this initiative flourish in Qatar. Your expertise is invaluable."

His proposition hung in the air, heavy with unspoken implications. Priya's heart raced, torn between the promise of professional fulfillment and the undeniable chemistry sparking between them.

But beneath the surface of her excitement lay trepidation. Could she trust him with her ambitions? And did her instincts scream louder about the risks than the exhilaration of possibility? Just then, Priya's phone buzzed, jolting her from her thoughts. An incoming message from Rohan read:

> Late meeting tonight. Hope all is well.

That one message threw a spotlight on the emotional conflict brewing beneath their professional overtures. She felt the walls closing in, the stark reality of her dual life crashing down like a wave.

Still standing close to Zayed, his eyes searching hers, Priya realized she was dancing on the edge, caught between a future filled with potential and the unrelenting grip of her responsibilities at home. The electric tension crackled in the night air, and in that ambiguous moment, she wondered if every decision, every conversation, would lead her closer to her destiny—or to her doom.

7
Chasing Shadows

Increased Frequency of Meetings

The air was charged with an electric anticipation each time Priya and Zayed found themselves in the same room. Meetings that once revolved around academic discussions or medical advancements now danced around the silent pulse of their connection, a rhythmic heartbeat that quickened with each glance shared between them. The confines of their professional interactions blurred, pushing them closer, making it increasingly difficult to ignore the budding intimacy that both excited and terrified Priya.

Zayed's charming demeanor rarely failed to draw Priya in, but what began as a harmless admiration morphed into something far more profound. He had become not just a colleague but a refuge from the hollowness that seeped into her everyday life. Their conversations, sprinkled with subtle flirtations, were now peppered with laughter and shared vulnerabilities, slipping seamlessly into the dangerously intoxicating territory of friendship that hovered just above the forbidden.

Yet, on one fateful evening, as twilight cast a soft glow over the city of Doha, their laughter faded into an unsettling silence. They stood inches apart, the distance between them charged with emotions that felt too heavy to be contained. Zayed glanced at Priya, his eyes revealing an intensity that made her heart race. Just as her lips parted to voice an uncharacteristic daring thought, the sudden buzz of Zayed's phone broke the moment. He stepped back, his expression torn, and as he answered the call, Priya felt an insatiable ache to breach the invisible barrier between them. The urgency to know what he was feeling, to throw caution to the wind and succumb to the desire that simmered beneath the surface, compelled her forward, yet she remained rooted to the spot, a prisoner of their circumstances.

As Zayed ended the call, his brow furrowed slightly, and Priya's heart plummeted. His demeanor shifted, clouded by the weight of unsaid things—his marital obligations, the legacy of family expectations looming like dark clouds overhead. With each occurrence, bitterness rose in her throat; she wanted to scream, to fight against the constraints holding them both captive. But as he stepped toward her, concern etched into his features, it became painfully clear that this delicately crafted connection was poised on a precipice. Their meetings had grown unbearable, a double-edged sword cutting deeper with every encounter. The intoxicating bliss they shared was tainted by the undeniable truth lurking behind their furtive smiles: the world outside their bubble was tearing at the seams, and reality demanded to be acknowledged.

Time felt suspended as Priya struggled between the lure of possibility and the impending threat looming over them. Would they tarnish the fragile beauty they had woven through secrecy, or confront the reality that stood between them? In that moment, she understood that a decision awaited—a choice that would either bind them in an exhilarating narrative of forbidden romance or shatter their world altogether. The closer they drew to the crescendo of their relationship, the more inevitable it became that they would have to confront the shadows of their desires and the consequences that came with them.

Navigating Marital Responsibilities

As Priya settled into her routine at the bustling hospital, her mind often drifted to the unexpected flicker of connection she had felt with Zayed. Each day felt like a balancing act, her responsibilities as a physician demanding her focus while the echoes of their shared moments pulled at her heart. Rohan, her husband, provided stability, yet the absence of passion in their marriage loomed like a haunting shadow over her soul. He was a reliable partner, a comforting presence, but Priya yearned for a depth of connection that remained just out of reach.

In the quiet moments after her shifts, she grappled with the weight of her marital obligations. The boundaries between duty and desire blurred as she recalled Zayed's warm gaze, their conversations rich with understanding and the kind of laughter that seemed to ignite a spark within her. Priya felt torn between the life she had chosen and the thrill of something that had blossomed unexpectedly. Could she acknowledge her feelings for Zayed without unraveling the ties that bound her to Rohan?

Meanwhile, Zayed's evenings were filled with the expectations of family obligations and societal functions. Sheikha Fatima, his wife, moved gracefully through their lives together, a beacon of strength in a world gilded with wealth and tradition. Yet beneath the surface, Zayed wrestled with silent frustrations, his heart echoing the same discontent Priya felt. The responsibilities he embraced often overshadowed the dreams and desires hidden within him. He wanted to honor his marriage, yet the allure of Priya called to him like a siren's song.

As their meetings increased, lingering between laughter and meaningful conversations, both struggled to navigate the responsibilities that loomed from their respective marriages. The excitement of new feelings came with the bittersweet burden of duty. Priya found herself constantly checking her phone, the anticipation of a message from Zayed intertwining with guilt as thoughts of her own husband whispered doubt into her mind. Was it fair to feel so alive with someone new while she was still entwined in her commitments at home?

The tension mounted like a taut string, and every moment shared felt like a stolen treasure, yet both knew the risks involved. Emotional entanglements grew deeper, and despite the barriers around them, the undeniable connection blurred the lines drawn by societal expectations. They stood on the precipice of choice, where a single step could send them crashing into chaos or, perhaps, free them to pursue the love they secretly craved.

As they exchanged sweet words and stolen glances, neither could ignore the storm brewing on the horizon. Priya's heart raced with both excitement and fear, a dichotomy that left her breathless. Would they choose to embrace the shadows of their desires, risking everything for a connection that felt both thrilling and taboo? The thought lingered like a promise, both richly enticing and dangerously precarious, with the weight of their responsibilities pressing heavily on their shoulders. The tension swirled quietly around them, a magnetic pull drawing them closer, yet threatening to unravel the very fabric of their lives.

Emotional Turmoil

The air between Priya and Zayed crackled with unspoken words, an electricity that neither of them fully understood but both felt deeply. Each meeting had transformed into a clandestine dance of longing and guilt, drawing them closer yet shackling them with the weight of their realities. Their frequent rendezvous had birthed a bond that transcended simple companionship—what had begun as professional respect now loomed like a dark forest, filled with shadows of desire and fear.

Priya often found herself staring at the opulent skyline of Doha, the glittering skyscrapers a stark contrast to her mundane life in Mumbai. Zayed's laughter echoed in her mind, his warmth enveloping her as she contemplated their last encounter. He had touched her hand, a lingering brush of skin that awakened something dormant within her—a yearning she had long suppressed.

The responsibilities of her life, her marriage to Rohan, suddenly felt constraining, as if a vise were tightening around her heart whenever she thought of the life she had chosen versus the one she secretly craved.

In the dim recesses of her soul, Priya wrestled with the implications of her emotions. Could she allow herself to fall into this abyss of connection with Zayed? Did her heart have the capacity for such dangerous love? She knew the answer—she was falling, inexorably. Each fleeting glance they shared at the conference sent ripples through her, igniting a fire that had long been extinguished. Zayed's presence was like an intoxicating potion, drawing her in, challenging everything she believed about her duties as a wife and a doctor.

On a sun-soaked afternoon, Zayed had taken her on a private tour of his foundation, showing her the impact of his philanthropic work. As he spoke passionately about the healthcare initiatives aimed at helping underprivileged families, Priya felt herself being pulled deeper into his world, the richness of his ideals blending beautifully with the stark reality of her life. Yet, with every shared laughter and intimate conversation, an undercurrent of anguish flowed. She recalled the warmth of Rohan's embrace, the stability he offered, as reality loomed like a dark shadow over her budding love for Zayed.

As she stood by the large windows overlooking the bustling streets of Doha that evening, Priya felt tears prick at the corners of her eyes, reflecting the dichotomy of joy and despair raging within her. The weight of her secret lay heavy on her shoulders, a secret that could rupture her world and leave devastation in its wake. Zayed had sent her a message earlier that day, a simple invitation to dinner. Her heart raced at the thought—it was both a temptation and a curse.

With every heartbeat, the chasm between her desires and her duties widened. Should she attend? Could she jettison the expectations that familial bonds and societal norms had tied around her? But as the moon ascended into the night sky, casting its silvery light across the city, Priya felt herself teetering on the brink of a decision that could shatter her carefully cultivated existence. Just then, the sound of her phone vibrating on the table brought her crashing back to reality—a text from Rohan.

It was a simple inquiry:

When will you be home?

Yet it struck her like a lightning bolt. The warmth of his words contrasted sharply with the cold reality of her secret rendezvous with Zayed.

Panic shot through her veins. What was she doing? The turmoil within her surged, a tempest threatening to erupt as she wrestled with an insatiable longing and a burgeoning sense of dread. If she said yes to Zayed, what would she be sacrificing? If she kept denying her heart, what kind of life awaited her? As the tensions mounted, Priya realized she stood at a crossroads

where every choice bore unimaginable consequences.

She picked up the phone, her fingers hovering over the keys, wrestling with the heaviness in her chest. Could she truly choose
the life that fulfilled her heart over the one
that had defined her? Each second felt like
an eternity as she fought against the pull of
emotional chaos raging inside her, a storm
of desire that threatened to sweep her
away. And yet, somewhere in the depths of
her mind, a small voice whispered: Life was
about to change—one way or another.

8
Window to New Worlds

Zayed's Warm Invitation

As the sun dipped below the horizon, casting an ethereal glow over the bustling cityscape of Doha, Zayed stood by the large glass windows of his office, feeling a restlessness within. The conference had sparked something inside him—this sense of connection with someone who, like him, was navigating the intricate dance of professional dedication and personal longing. Priya Sharma... the name resonated with a warmth that was both thrilling and terrifying.

It was during the coffee break, the scent of freshly brewed espresso filling the air, that Zayed found himself drawn towards her once more. He had observed the way her eyes sparkled with passion and intelligence as she spoke about her medical research. It was a stark contrast to the stifled conversations filled with expectations he was accustomed to. That familiarity with his own discontent pulled him towards her, as if the universe conspired to blur the lines between their worlds. As he approached her, he felt an unfamiliar thrill—a tingling electricity that made time momentarily halt.

"Priya," he said, his voice calm despite the quickening beat of his heart. "I would love for you to see some of the philanthropic work my foundation is involved with. It's more than just numbers and reports; it's about changing lives."

The invitation hung in the air, heavy with implications, but laced with an undeniable promise. Priya's expression shifted swiftly from surprise to intrigue, and in that moment, Zayed sensed the gravity of his words bearing down on both of them.

As she considered his proposal, a flicker of hesitation crossed her face. The weight of her obligations tugged at her mind, yet curiosity danced in her eyes.

"I'd appreciate that, Zayed. It would be enlightening to witness firsthand," she replied, her voice steady but her heart racing with the excitement of the unknown.

Days melted into nights, yet their connection remained vibrant in his mind, like a flame flickering in the dark. When the moment finally came for her to visit, Zayed meticulously prepared for her arrival, the anticipation sending ripples of excitement through his composed exterior. He envisioned showing Priya the projects that truly mattered—the initiatives that reflected the values he held dear, merging their lives through meaningful conversations.

But the deeper truth lurked beneath the surface. As they navigated the sprawling city, with every shared glance and every laughter-filled moment, an invisible thread pulled tighter between them. Zayed was acutely aware of the boundary that divided their lives—marriages that represented duty but felt like cages—yet with each interaction, he found himself yearning for more than just fleeting banter.

That day in Doha would not merely be an exploration of philanthropic endeavors;

it was a doorway to a world where they could discover each other deeper than ever before. Yet, with this invitation lay a storm brewing on the horizon—the uncharted territories of their hearts fraught with complications, where every moment spent together flared into something more tumultuous, something that could not be contained within the confines of mere professional interest.

As the sun dipped low, casting an enchanting glow on the city, Priya and Zayed stepped into each other's worlds, the echoes of their decisions resonating with secrets yet to be revealed. And as the shadows grew longer, so too did the tension between longing and duty, the tug-of-war between what was expected and what was felt, igniting the anticipation of an encounter that would challenge the very foundation of their lives.

A Day in Doha

As the morning sun began its ascent over the soaring skyline of Doha, Priya found herself standing at the threshold of an unfamiliar world. The vibrant city, a confluence of modernity and tradition, buzzed with life. Zayed, ever the gracious host, watched her with an eagerness that mirrored her own curiosity. This was not just a visit; it felt like the unguarded opening of a door into a reality that had always seemed beyond her reach.

They began their day at the Souq Waqif, where the scent of spices intertwined with the rich aroma of Arabic coffee. The market was a labyrinth of colors and sounds, enveloping her senses in a way that felt intoxicating. Zayed's enthusiasm was infectious as he pointed out various stalls, discussing the history and significance behind each artifact. Priya listened intently, captivated not only by the stories but also by the passion that radiated from him. His happiness brought a warmth that felt wholly inviting, and it was in these moments that she began to let down her walls, if only slightly.

Over the next few hours, they discovered hidden gems of the city. A visit to a local art gallery in the Souq opened her eyes to the contemporary artist's worldview, blending tradition and modern artistry in unexpected ways. As Zayed explained his foundation's support for burgeoning talents in Qatar, Priya saw the man beyond the business mogul— a man who cared deeply about nurturing creativity and making a real dif-ference. She found herself drawn to him in ways that felt both exhilarating and forbid-den, her heart racing at the thought of their burgeoning connection.

Yet, with every passing moment, an un-spoken tension lingered between them, a reminder of the boundaries they were inch-ing closer to crossing. When Zayed took her hand as they navigated through the twisted alleys of the old Souq, it felt natural, yet perilous. A simple gesture, but one charged with a gravity that electrified the air around them. Her pulse quickened, a mixture of anticipation and fear. Was she really prepared to delve deeper into this unexpected relationship? Would embracing this connection mean risking everything she had built? The questions spiraled in her mind, colliding with the intoxicating energy of their day together.

As the sun began to dip below the horizon, painting the sky in shades of orange and pink, they found themselves at a quiet terrace in the Pearl overlooking the Arabian Gulf. The picturesque view was breathtaking, but it was Zayed's piercing gaze that captivated her most. In that moment, time seemed to stand still. He spoke softly, sharing his dreams and fears, baring his soul in a way that made her heart swell. She could feel the weight of his words, the depth of his longing for something real amidst the facades they both maintained in their lives.

But with the depth of connection came

the stark reality lingering in the back of her mind. The world they inhabited was structured by duty and expectation, caught between the layers of tradition and modernity. Priya's heart warred with her mind, torn between the magnetic pull toward Zayed and the responsibilities that awaited her back in India. As Zayed leaned closer, their faces barely inches apart, she felt the air shift. The gravity of their growing attraction felt palpable, a force pulling them together yet warning of the dangers that could ensue.

"We really shouldn't," she whispered, the plea escaping her lips before she could think twice.

The intensity in Zayed's eyes reflected a mixture of understanding and desire, yet behind the allure danced the shadow of consequence. In that fleeting moment, Priya realized that she stood at the precipice of a decision that would shape the course of their lives forever. The question now echoed in her mind: would she take the leap into the unknown or step back into the life that felt increasingly hollow?

Priya's Life: Stories and Struggles

Priya sat in the plush, sunlit office of the Doha hospital, her heart still racing from her recent encounter with Zayed. The vibrant colors of the cityscape outside were a stark contrast to the subdued grays of her life back in Mumbai. She thought about the stories she had been told during her upbringing—of strong women who sacrificed their ambitions for love and family. Each tale echoed within her now, urging her to confront the reality of her own life.

Her thoughts drifted back to Rohan, her husband, the man she had respected and cared for deeply, yet felt an invisible wall between them. Their evenings blurred into a routine of quiet dinners and gentle nods, their conversations devoid of the spark she so desperately craved. As much as she wanted to rewrite the narrative, she couldn't help but feel trapped within the story written for her.

"What do you want, Priya?" she whispered to herself, the question lingering like an uninvited guest in her mind. She realized it wasn't merely the thrill of Zayed's presence that captivated her; it was the profound sense of being seen, of being understood. As the sun dipped below the horizon, casting shadows across her thoughts, she knew she had to share her struggles with Zayed—perhaps that would lay the groundwork for what she hoped could be something more.

When she finally found the courage to let her guard down, she was surprised at how easily the words flowed.

"I've always been told to put others first," she confessed, a heaviness lifting slightly from her chest. Zayed listened intently, his unwavering gaze encouraging her to continue. "But in doing so, I feel like I've lost pieces of myself. I feel like a ghost sometimes, drifting through my days without purpose."

Zayed's expression softened, his empathy palpable.

"You deserve to be heard, to chase your dreams," he replied, his voice low and reassuring.

This connection, fraught with unspoken tension, was a lifeline for Priya—an unexpected intertwining of their lives that filled her with both exhilaration and fear.

Yet, as their conversations deepened, she couldn't shake the gnawing doubt that danced at the edges of her mind. What could come of this connection if they continued to explore it? The challenge of navigating their individual circumstances loomed large, like a shadow cast over the bright potential of their emerging bond. The closer they drew, the tighter the web of complications around them became.

The room felt smaller as she uttered her next words:

"But can we really be open about our desires? What will it mean for our families?"

She searched Zayed's face for answers, for a promise that they could defy their destinies without drawing an end to everything they held dear.

"The world is not as rigid as it appears," he said, a flicker of determination lighting his eyes. "But it might cost us—more than we can imagine."

There was a weight in his voice, a horizon full of both danger and hope. Priya's heart raced, recognizing the crossroads they stood at, caught in a moment that felt powerful yet precarious. Would she dare to leap into this new world with Zayed or retreat back into the familiar shadows of her life? The risks were palpable and echoed in her deepest fears.

Just then, the door swung open, interrupting their fervent exchange. A nurse rushed in, her face a mask of urgency, shattering the cocoon of intimacy they had woven.

"Dr. Priya, there's been an emergency in the ER," she announced breathlessly. "We need you now."

Priya's heart sank as reality crashed back in. The moment of reckoning was snatched away, leaving her with a swirling mix of desire and dread.

As she stood to follow the nurse, Zayed's hand caught hers lightly, a fleeting touch that ignited the tension between them once more.

"We will revisit this," he whispered, urgency threading through his words.

Priya felt the pull of destiny. Every step towards the ER felt heavy with the weight of choice—between the familiarity of her past and the thrilling unknown of her future, where the potential of love awaited. In that moment, she realized that some choices could change the very fabric of who she was. But was she ready to pay the price?

9
Unspoken Desires

Tension in the Air

A PALPABLE TENSION ENVELOPED the crowded conference hall as Priya maneuvered through throngs of attendees, her mind racing with thoughts of Zayed. Since their chance encounter, the magnetic pull between them had only intensified, filling the space between their words with unspoken desires and muted glances. She could feel his presence even when they were apart, an electric charge lingering in the air, drawing her closer to him despite the invisible barriers that tradition and duty erected around them.

Zayed stood at the edge of the auditorium, his poised demeanor belying the turmoil brewing within. He had watched Priya engage with her colleagues, her laughter resonating like music against the backdrop of formal discussions and presentations. Each smile she shared felt like a silent invitation, igniting a fire within him that had long been dormant. He was caught between his responsibilities towards Sheikha Fatima and their children and this undeniable connection that flared brighter with each fleeting moment spent with Priya. Every unguarded look exchanged between them was a reminder of what they risked losing—a profound and exhilarating bond suppressed by the expectations of their worlds.

As the applause faded, Priya locked eyes with Zayed, an electrifying connection sparking between them, sending a rush of adrenaline coursing through her veins. It was then that the tension reached a breaking point, an invisible thread pulling them further into each other's orbit, refusing to loosen its grip. This moment, cloaked in a mixture of exhilaration and anxiety, felt both serendipitous and forbidden, a testament to the complexity of their desires. The air around them thickened, and time hung precariously in the balance as their shared attraction teetered on the brink of something undefined and potentially cataclysmic.

Just as they thought they might bridge the chasm between them, a familiar voice jolted Zayed from his reverie, reminding him of the world that awaited them outside the conference walls. It was Sheikha Fatima, her presence a sharp counterpoint to the desire that shimmered in the air. Zayed turned, the moment shattered, as he grappled with the weight of his choices and the consequences that loomed like dark clouds on the horizon. The very fabric of their lives was woven from secrets and expectations, yet all he could think of was the enchanting allure of what could be. Would they dare to navigate this storm together, or would the unspoken desires between them remain just that—unspoken?

Confessions of the Heart

A palpable tension existed in the air, heavy with unspoken words and desires that buzzed like electricity between Priya and Zayed. They stood on the balcony of the hotel overlooking the glittering skyline of Dubai, their breaths mingling with the cool evening breeze. It felt as if the world around them had faded, leaving only the two of them suspended in a moment that defied their realities. Priya's heart raced as she glanced at Zayed, his eyes reflecting not just the city lights but the depth of emotion that lay beneath his composed exterior.

"Do you ever wonder what it would be like to abandon everything? To live without the constraints of duty and expectation?" Zayed ventured, his voice a whisper that seemed to echo in the stillness.

Priya's heart fluttered. His words resonated deep within her, sparking a yearning she had buried for so long. She looked away, her mind racing with the implications of his question, the weight of her own life pressing down on her.

"Every day," she admitted, her voice shaky, "I feel trapped in a life that isn't completely mine. There's a part of me that craves more—more passion, more connection."

She risked a glance at him, and the vulnerability in Zayed's gaze made her pulse quicken. They were daring to speak the unspeakable, to voice desires that had remained hidden for too long. It was exhilarating and terrifying all at once.

As the last rays of sun dipped below the horizon, painting the sky in hues of crimson and indigo, Zayed took a step closer, reducing the distance that felt both exhilarating and perilous.

"Priya, I can't pretend that this connection isn't real. I feel it, too. There's something deeply magnetic about what we have."

The intensity in his voice sent shivers down her spine, igniting a fire within her that had long been extinguished.

The world seemed to vanish as she searched his eyes for answers she had perhaps already known. She wanted to confess the depth of her feelings, to lay bare the desires that had blossomed like wildflowers in her heart. But fear clawed at her; the consequences felt overwhelming, shifting like shadows in the twilight.

"Zayed, we..." she started, but the words caught in her throat.

What are we doing? The weight of the question hung between them like a pendulum ticking toward an inevitable climax. They both understood that crossing this line would come with consequences, potential heartbreak, and the haunting specter of betrayal to their spouses who trusted them. Yet, the tension in the air felt more like an invitation than a warning.

"What if we don't overthink it?" Zayed suggested, his voice low, emboldened by the proximity of their bodies, "What if we just let ourselves feel?"

His words lingered in the air, dangerously tempting. Something deep inside Priya surged, a longing that muddied her thoughts and blurred her moral compass. All the joys and the sorrows she stored away within herself screamed for release.

As silence enveloped them, both were left grappling with their desires. The thrill of their connection flickered with the promise of something beautiful yet utterly dangerous. Zayed moved closer, his presence pulling her in like a moth to a flame. In that charged moment, they stood at the precipice, ready to leap into the unknown, aware that whatever lay beyond would redefine everything they once knew.

"Tell me you feel it, too," Zayed urged, his breath mingling with hers, creating a cocoon around them that felt both safe and electrifying.

Priya's heart pounded, caught between the conflicting tides of her reality and her yearning. The intensity of the moment pulled her forward, yet hesitation tethered her feet to the ground. With a deep inhale, she prepared to speak her truth, unsure if she was ready for what might follow.

Across the dusky Dubai skyline, the stars began to twinkle, witnessing the pivotal moment that would carry them into the depths of uncharted territories, as Priya leaned closer, ready to confess the desires that had long been whispered in the corners of her heart.

Consequences of Attraction

The air was thick with an unspoken tension as Priya and Zayed stood facing each other, the world around them fading into a distant hum. Their recent confessions hung between them like an unyielding challenge, forcing them to confront the undeniable bond that had formed in such a short time. The conference buzzed around them, yet they were insulated, cocooned in their own universe where every glance felt charged with longing.

In the intimacy of shared secrets, the consequences of their attraction began to crystallize, the beauty of their connection contrasted starkly against the peril it entailed. Each heartbeat echoed the gravity of their situation—behind Zayed lay the elaborate tapestry of his family name, the weight of tradition tugging at his shoulders, while Priya's heart wrenched at the thought of the family she promised to nurture and the husband she respected yet felt so distant from.

The lingering kisses shared in the silence of their minds were held against the backdrop of their duties—Zayed, the dutiful husband to Sheikha Fatima, tasked with maintaining his family's honor; Priya, the committed physician, often tethered to her responsibilities, but also yearning for a love that filled the void in her heart. As they exchanged lingering glances, the reality of their emotional entanglement began to weave its intricate web, threatening to ensnare them both. Would they continue down this path, risking everything, or would they retreat into the safety of the lives they had built and the promises made to others?

With each heartbeat, a decision loomed—a decision that would carry ripples far beyond the uneasy tranquility of this moment. Priya's thoughts spiraled as she weighed the thrilling prospects of abandoning her constraints, feeling alive for the first time against the backdrop of the rigid life she'd constructed. Zayed's eyes, filled with sincerity and a hint of desperation, mirrored her own turmoil as he quietly dared to hope for a future stripped of traditional dictates. Their shared pulse seemed to synchronize, echoing a longing that danced on the precipice of sheer chaos.

But a noise pierced their reverie, an unwelcome reminder of reality—the sound of laughter, vibrant and careless, pulled Zayed's focus momentarily toward the group of conference attendees nearby, their joviality starkly contrasting the weight of their unspoken desires. Priya glanced at him, her breath catching as she registered the shift, the flicker of hesitation in his eyes. The magnetism of attraction was mingling dangerously with doubt, and the confluence of emotions threatened to unleash a tempest if left unchecked.

As Zayed's gaze fell back to hers, something unyielding crystallized in the space between them. Both were acutely aware that the beauty of what they had discovered was inextricably tied to perilous consequences. The future felt taut with possibility and heartache—a fragile balance that might shatter at the slightest push. They could feel it, the weight of their choices bearing down as they stood on the edge of something both intoxicating and terrifying.

This clandestine connection offered warmth against the coldness of their realities, yet it came with risks that could unravel their lives. They would need to tread carefully, navigating the narrow path between forbidden desires and the expectations of their worlds. Perhaps it would be mere moments before the delicate equilibrium was disrupted, the consequences of their attraction breaking forth in a tumultuous wave. Suddenly, the journey ahead felt less like a choice and more like an inevitable plunge into the depths of passion and possibility, where the unspoken could either unify or destroy.

10
Breaking the Barriers

A Moment of Weakness

Underneath the dazzling chandelier of the grand ballroom, filled with laughter and the clinking of crystal glasses, the world around Priya and Zayed melted away. They had spent weeks navigating their feelings, circling each other like moths drawn to a flame, caught in a dance of unspoken attraction. The thrill of their connection held an excitement that was both intoxicating and terrifying.

As the evening progressed, the air thickened with the weight of their unsaid desires. Priya caught Zayed's gaze, that familiar spark illuminating their surroundings, igniting the emotions they had cautiously tended. In that moment, the bustling crowd faded, leaving only the two of them suspended in time. Her heart raced, a tempest of longing battling against the reality of their circumstances. In a bid to dissipate the tension, she laughed at a shared joke, her voice dancing between them, inviting him closer.

Zayed inched nearer, the fragrance of his cologne enveloping Priya like a gentle embrace. His warm presence sent shivers down her spine.

"This feels unreal, doesn't it?" he whispered, the softness of his voice laced with vulnerability.

Priya nodded, her breath hitching as they teetered on the brink of something monumental. What had begun as a professional admiration spiraled into an emotional whirlwind, threatening to consume them both.

With the rhythm of distant music pulsating in the background, he reached for her hand, intertwining their fingers—a forbidden act that sent electric currents through her body. This simple gesture unleashed a torrent of emotions she had been battling to suppress. In that fleeting moment, they were not defined by their obligations, their spouses, or the expectations of their families. They were just two souls yearning for connection, bound together by the artifice of circumstance.

"I shouldn't..." Priya started, but the words felt feeble, drowned out by the chaos of her emotions.

Zayed's eyes searched hers, fervent and intense—questions, hopes, and fears swirled in that gaze.

"Sometimes, moments of weakness reveal our true selves, Priya," he told her, his thumb gently stroking her hand, igniting a fire that burned through every rational thought in her mind.

She could feel her heart pounding in response, the intensity of the moment cascading over her like a wave.

"What if we are making a mistake?" she breathed, uncertainty clinging to her words even as desire eclipsed reason.

Zayed drew closer, his breath warm against her ear, and as he whispered:

"What if this is exactly what we need?"

Priya closed her eyes, grappling with the chaos that raged within her. Could she truly let herself surrender to a connection so profound yet fraught with peril?

In that essence of vulnerability, they crossed an invisible line, one that sealed their fates together while igniting an emotional inferno. Zayed leaned in, their lips almost touching, awakening feelings she had long buried—a moment of weakness felt like a reckless plunge into the depths of forbidden waters. A decision was dancing on the tip of her tongue, and yet, the shadows of their consequences loomed large. At that instant, Priya realized the gravity of what awaited them beyond this moment of surrender.

As if reading her thoughts, Zayed pulled back slightly, his brows furrowing with concern, making the tension crackle in the air around them.

"Priya…" he began, but before he could finish, the sound of laughter erupted nearby, shattering the fragile bubble they had created.

The moment hung heavy, leaving them

teetering on the cusp of discovery, and Priya's heart raced with the knowledge that their shared secret was at risk of exposure. Could they really tread this dangerous path without losing everything they held dear?

Crossing Emotional Boundaries

In the soft, muted light of dawn, Priya and Zayed found an unexpected sanctuary in a quiet corner of the sprawling conference hall, a temporary escape from the sharp glare of the world outside. The air was thick with unspoken words, both acutely aware of the fissures forming between their professional facades and personal yearnings. Gone was the crisp barrier of formality they had once maintained—what lingered now was a heady mix of curiosity and desire.

"There's something about the way you speak about your work," Zayed said, his voice low, drawing Priya closer into the intimacy of his presence. "You're passionate, and yet... it feels like there's so much more you are meant to explore."

His dark eyes held hers, a keen intensity that sent a shiver down her spine. She felt seen in a way she hadn't for years—a stark contrast to the silent void in her marriage, where Rohan's kind but unchallenging demeanor had left her feeling stifled.

Priya's heart raced as she considered the implication of his words, a stifling uncertainty swirling within her. How could she possibly embrace this connection when every moment spent with Zayed felt like standing on the precipice of something forbidden?

"I've always been driven, perhaps too much so," she replied, her voice barely above a whisper. "But this—what we're doing—it's crossing lines that I..." She faltered, the weight of their hidden emotions hitting her like a freight train.

"I don't want to rush," Zayed offered, his gaze softening, but the tension in his body belied his intention.

With each passing second, the boundaries she had carefully constructed around her heart began to fray. The chemistry between them thrummed with the potential for both ecstasy and destruction.

"Yet, sometimes, it feels as though we are

meant to feel this connection."

Words hung heavy in the air, swirling like leaves caught in an autumn gust. Priya felt drawn to him, their worlds colliding amidst the backdrop of duty and expectation. In that brief, stolen moment, she longed to reach out, to bridge the chasm that loomed between them. But in doing so, she risked not only her own happiness but the lives they had built around their respective responsibilities—lives laden with obligations and societal confines.

A sudden noise—a group of colleagues passing by—startled them back to reality. Priya's heart plummeted, awareness of the external world flooding back, and with it, the clarity of their precarious situation.

"We should... we should get back," she stammered, breaking the spell, her cheeks burning as she stepped back, gathering her composure like a lifeline.

Zayed hesitated, the pulse of tension still palpable between them, and she could see the struggle in his eyes, mirrored perfectly in her own.

"Priya," he started, but she held up a hand, her pulse racing.

"Not now," she implored, fear gnawing at her insides.

The space they had occupied moments before felt like a world without consequence, but now the stakes felt irrevocably high. They returned to the conference, though the thunder of their hearts contrasted with the mundane discussions around them. Each glance exchanged felt electric; the rush of unspoken feelings between them pulsed like a haunting melody, begging for release.

As the day continued, Priya's focus wavered. Zayed was a constant presence in the periphery of her mind, an ever-growing distraction. The thin wall separating them had begun to erode, leaving her to question her choices and her life with Rohan. Yet, the prospect of crossing into this new territory was laden with potential heartbreak, every heartbeat echoing the conflict deep within her soul. She could almost taste the sweet allure of what could be, but it teetered on the edge of peril. It was a dangerous game they played, and as the sun began to dip below the horizon, casting long shadows over the bustling conference halls, Priya couldn't shake the feeling that they were standing at the brink of everything she had ever known.

Shared Secrets

In the stillness of the Dubai night, Priya and Zayed found themselves separated by mere inches yet encircled by the weight of unspoken emotions. Their shared vulnerability in that hushed hotel suite felt like an unseen thread binding them tighter with each lingering moment. The city outside pulsed with life, but within these walls, their world felt suspended in time, swirling around the secret they had both acknowledged yet feared.

Every brush of Zayed's fingers against her skin sent shivers racing through Priya's body, awakening senses dulled by the mundane rhythm of her life back in Mumbai. She yearned for this connection, this electric spark that promised to bridge the cultural divide and personal expectations that had encumbered them for far too long. Yet, the reality of their lives loomed like a storm cloud, threatening to pour its relentless rain at any moment—one wrong word, one slip of the tongue—and everything could unravel.

"What are we doing, Zayed?" Priya finally whispered, the tremor in her voice belying her composed facade.

She pulled back slightly, searching his eyes for clarity amid the confusion swirling inside her. The sincerity mirrored there stoked the fire of uncertainty within her, igniting thoughts of her stable yet passionless marriage to Rohan and Zayed's responsibilities weighing upon his successful empire.

Zayed inhaled deeply, and she could see the internal battle he waged—a man trapped between duty and desire, each heartbeat an agonizing reminder of the committed lives they led.

"I don't know," he confessed, whispering into the space that seemed to be thick with expectation. "But I feel it, Priya. I feel something real, something that transcends our worlds."

His words, heavy with longing, both

thrilled and terrified her.

The closeness between them was intoxicating but fraught with consequences that could shatter everything. As Zayed reached for her, cupping her cheek, the dissonance between society's expectations and the happiness they found in each other echoed loudly. She flinched at the sheer weight of the decision looming over them—a precipice from which they could either plunge into the depths of unknown joy or spiral down into chaos and despair.

Pulses raced, thoughts collided, and then came the sudden sound of a notification on Zayed's phone, breaking their intimate cocoon. Both their hearts raced as he glanced at the screen, the tension of shared secrets morphing into a palpable dread that settled in the pit of Priya's stomach. Rohan's name illuminated the screen, stark proof of the life they would be risking should this moment spiral out of control.

"I should answer," Zayed muttered, his voice strained, knowing that the slightest hint of this bond could ignite a wildfire they could never extinguish.

Before she could voice her protest, he swiped the screen, the light of his phone dimly reflecting the two lives they each had sworn to uphold. The room felt smaller now, the air heavier. She wanted nothing more than to pull him back into her world, away from the specter of obligations, away from the chains that would seek to keep them apart. But the line drawn between desires and responsibilities appeared more pronounced with each tick of the clock.

As Zayed pressed a number to connect with Rohan, all pieces of their shared secret—their emotions, their growing bond, and their desperate longing—clashed violently in her mind. Somewhere, among the chaos of their feelings lay the roots of their potential downfall, and Priya felt as if they stood on the brink of revelation, a pendulum swinging that could either gift them the freedom to love or plunge them into irrevocable darkness.

11
The Weight of Choices

Return to Normalcy

As Priya stepped through the threshold of her home in Mumbai, the familiar scent of spices and freshly washed linens met her like an embrace, yet it felt eerily distant. Rohan was in the living room, engrossed in his usual evening routine – the television flickering images of a world that seemed utterly disconnected from the whirlwind of emotions Priya had just navigated. Sitting beside him, she felt both comforted and suffocated by the mundane rhythm of her life, the stark juxtaposition of her recent experiences in Dubai clashing against her predictably serene existence. Each passing moment weighed heavily upon her, a reminder of the tantalizing freedom she had felt even if just for a heartbeat.

The laughter of their neighbors drifted in from the open window, a joyful sound that twisted the knife of longing deeper into her heart. Her thoughts drifted back to Zayed

– the way his laughter danced like sunlight through a canopy of trees, illuminating the hidden corners of her soul that had long been shrouded in shadow. The conversations they shared were etched in her mind, each word a fragile thread pulling her away from the life she had always known. Priya's heart flared with painful longing whenever she thought of the electrifying connection they had forged, a contrast so vivid against her routine life that it felt almost cruel. She loved the predictability of her existence, yet it now felt like a cage, with its bars woven from the very fabric of her own choices.

The evening passed slowly as Priya put on a brave face, engaging in small talk with Rohan, who appeared blissfully unaware of the tempest brewing within her. As the reality of her day-to-day responsibilities settled back in, a gnawing sense of guilt swept over her. The intimacy she had tasted with Zayed was a stark reminder of all she felt was missing, as if the universe had shown her a glimpse of something magnificent only to snatch it away, leaving her to grapple with her unfulfilled desires. She buried the thoughts deep within, developing a facade of normalcy, but the fragile threads of her commitment quivered in response, threatening to unravel.

Later that night, as she lay in bed, her mind raced. Each moment shared with Zayed fed the fire of her emotions, and she felt herself spiraling into a darkness of uncertainty. What price would her heart pay for the mere notion of happiness? Could she reconcile the growing void between herself and Rohan, who seemed unaware of the changes brewing within her? Yet, buried beneath her conflicts was an inkling of hope, a desire to reclaim the spark that had dimmed over the years.

Suddenly, the soft pings of her phone broke through the silence, sending a jolt of adrenaline racing through her. It was a message from Zayed, simple yet electrifying: Thinking of you. The words sent a rush of warmth flooding through her veins, a stark reminder that hidden within their choices was a blend of love and longing, of passion and pain. Suddenly, everything she thought she had returned to felt so fragile. The allure of their bond called to her once again; amidst the soothing sounds of a normal life, a shadow began to emerge – whispers of temptation lurking just below the surface, nudging her to revisit the passions stashed away in the corners of her heart.

As she tapped a response, her heart raced in her chest. What was she doing? Was she ready to dance upon the edge of that precipice again? The glow of her phone illuminated her face, and in that moment, she felt her reality tilting at an ever-increasing angle. With every keystroke, the ease and comfort of her ordinary life crumbled further, fanning flames she thought she could suppress. By the time she hit send, the line between normalcy and chaos had forever blurred, leaving her gasping at the weight of the choices that loomed ahead.

The Burden of Secrets

As the sun dipped below the horizon, casting a warm golden glow over the bustling city of Mumbai, Dr. Priya Sharma sat at her cluttered desk in the hospital, her mind miles away from the crumpled patient charts and medical journals. The weight of her recent encounter with Zayed lingered like a haunting melody, refusing to let her rest. She had returned to her normal life, the familiar beep of machines and the hurried footsteps of nurses providing a stark contrast to the enchantment of their time together in Dubai. Yet, the burden she bore felt increasingly insurmountable.

Meanwhile, across the desert sands in Qatar, Sheikh Zayed bin Sultan Al-Thani found himself ensnared in a web of unspoken truths and mounting anxiety. Every day at the office was an exercise in restraint. He had excelled at managing the expectations of his family and business associates, presenting a flawless facade. Yet, the shadow of his secret relationship with Priya loomed large, darkening even the brightest moments in his life. His heart raced at the thought of what their connection meant, the allure of their stolen moments giving way to a constant churn of guilt and fear.

As days turned into weeks, the tension of unspoken words became a silent scream that drowned out everything else. Both Priya and Zayed found themselves seeking solace in their work, pouring their energies into their respective careers as a means to escape the complexity of their emotions. But no amount of focus could uncouple them from the reality of their secret – a reality that held the potential to unravel not just their lives, but also the lives of those they cared for most.

What once felt exhilarating had trans-formed into a heavy burden; each glance at a text message sent or received across continents sparked both thrill and dread. The secrets they shared, laced with passion and desire, now felt like chains holding them captive. Priya had never imagined that love, when found, could feel so confining, so perilous. As she gazed out of her hospital window at the Mumbai skyline, the vibrant city contrasting sharply with her internal turmoil, her resolve wavered. Was the joy of the forbidden worth the pain of the inevitable fallout?

Across the ocean, Zayed sat in his office, staring at the horizon from his lavish window. The opulence of his surroundings felt suffocating against the backdrop of his choices. Each passing moment intensified his longing for Priya, but the walls seemed to close in around him. He pondered how many more nights he could weather this storm of secrets without surrendering to temptation or losing everything he had built. How long could they sustain this dual existence before something shattered the fragile peace they had created?

Just as the night began to fall heavy with unanswered questions, both Zayed and

Priya received a message that shattered the fragile illusion they had constructed. The words were simple yet explosive, sending shockwaves through their already tumultuous hearts: "We need to talk." This single line echoed like a siren's call, spiraling their emotions into chaos. The faces of their spouses loomed in their minds as the gravity of what lay ahead pressed upon them. Was the desire they fought so hard to keep secret about to explode into the unforgiving light of day? With a feeling of dread heavy in their stomachs, they braced themselves for the inevitable confrontation that could either cement their bond or destroy everything they held dear.

Seeking Solace in Work

Dr. Priya Sharma hurried through the bustling corridors of the Mumbai hospital, the hum of conversations and the beeping of monitors enveloping her like an old, comforting blanket. Each patient she treated was a reminder of the life she had dedicated herself to, yet a persistent ache within her heart whispered of the emptiness that awaited her at home. Rohan, her husband, was a kind man, but in their marriage, there was an absence of passion that felt increasingly suffocating. After her encounters with Sheikh Zayed, she had discovered a spark in herself that had long been dormant.

In stark contrast, Sheikh Zayed bin Sultan Al-Thani sat in his lavish office in Doha, the sunlight cascading through his expansive windows and catching the dust motes dancing in the air. He peered at the sprawling city beneath him, feeling an overwhelming weight on his shoulders—the legacy of wealth and tradition, the expectations of a family, and a partnership with Sheikha Fatima that left him yearning for connection. As he reviewed the proposed initiatives for his philanthropic foundation, his thoughts drifted to Priya, their burgeoning bond a distraction he desperately wanted to explore but couldn't.

Both found themselves retreating into their work as a refuge from their tangled emotions. For Priya, each surgical procedure was a testimony to her commitment and skill, a stark contrast to the chaos of her heart. Meanwhile, Zayed poured his passion into healthcare initiatives, trying to forge a path towards a future where he could reshape not only his country's health landscape but perhaps, in some twisted sense, his own destiny. Yet, despite their respective successes, an unshakeable solitude loomed large, amplifying their feelings of yearning and creating a fragile thread connecting them across vast distances.

As days turned into weeks, Priya stood

before a particularly challenging case—a young boy fighting the odds with unwavering spirit. Her focus narrowed, but with every stitch and incision, thoughts of Zayed infiltrated her mind. Could this connection be the answer to the yearning she had felt for so long, or was it merely a distraction from the life she had painstakingly built? In that moment, Zayed was not just a whisper in the back of her mind; he was the promise of something beyond the monotonous rhythm of her days.

Simultaneously, Zayed found himself preparing for a gala event intended to further his foundation's initiatives. The city lights glimmered like stars, but they paled in comparison to the spark Priya ignited within him. He shouldered the invisible mask of confidence and control, but inside, he wrestled with the simmering tension of their unknown future. Should he confess the depth of his feelings, knowing well the tidal wave of consequences such a revelation could unleash? As he stood ready to walk into the spotlight, he caught the echo of a soft laugh, a fleeting reminder of Priya's presence and how well she understood the fleeting nature of life and love.

That evening, as Priya scrubbed down after yet another twelve-hour shift, a buzzing message on her phone pulled her from the exhaustion. It was Zayed, a simple text that felt monumental.

> Thinking of you. How do I find solace in a life of expectations?

The query hung heavy in the air, and with every tap of her fingers against the screen, the weight of their choices began to descend like a storm cloud. Did she dare seek solace in him, or would she bury her longing beneath the mounting responsibilities that awaited her?

For both Priya and Zayed, their careers offered a semblance of control and fulfillment, yet they were perilously intertwined with the emotional chaos that brewed beneath the surface. As they strove to find refuge in their work, the very feelings they sought to escape only intensified the longing, leading them down a treacherous path where their next choices loomed large and irrevocable.

12
Yearning Across Miles

Long-Distance Connection

The days stretched on without Zayed, the distance between Mumbai and Doha like an invisible chasm carved through her heart. Priya's fingers grazed over her phone, resisting the urge to reach out. Each time they spoke, it felt like they were pushing against a tide of longing and trepidation.

In the quiet corners of her mind, she replayed the stolen moments they had shared—the laughter, the late-night confessions, the way he had looked at her as if she held the universe in her palms. Yet, beneath that swirl of affection lay an undercurrent of anxiety. What if they slipped too far into the abyss of their emotions? What if Rohan sensed that something was amiss? It was a risk that weighed heavily on her conscience.

As she prepared for another day at the hospital, her phone chimed—a message from Zayed, simple yet electric:

Thinking of you.

A warmth spread through her like sunlight breaking through autumn clouds, but the shadows followed close behind. Their connection, once thrilling, now felt intertwined with the specter of discovery. Each message, each call, intensified the strain on her heart, balancing on the precipice of hope and despair.

Priya found herself yearning for their conversations. They spoke of their work, their dreams, but the heartbreaking reality of their commitments always lingered. A flicker of doubt ignited within her. Was this longing worth the potential pain? The thought gnawed at her, gnashing like teeth against the fragile fabric of her everyday life.

As the sun dipped low, painting the sky with hues of orange and purple, Priya's phone buzzed again. Another message from Zayed, but this time the tone felt heavier, more urgent.

Can we talk? It's important.

The flutter of apprehension in her chest melded with concern. What could possibly be so important, especially under the ever-watchful eyes of their respective worlds?

She steeled herself for the conversation, her heart racing as she dialed his number. When his voice broke through the connection, rich and resonant, it sent shivers coursing down her spine. They talked as if the distance folded in on itself, but the weight of unspoken fear hung in the air.

"Priya," he began, his tone serious. "We can't keep living in this shadow."

The ominous echo of his words struck her like thunder, reverberating through the walls of her carefully constructed life.

Suddenly, the stakes felt perilously high. With every glance at the clock, the urgency of their situation pulsed. Their hearts, once jubilant in shared secrets, now collided with the danger of discovery looming ever closer. As distant stars twinkled outside her window, Priya could feel the tightening of a noose. They were dancing on the edge of a cliff, and she sensed the instability beneath her feet. Would they fall? Or could they somehow soar above the chaos that surrounded them?

The thought both thrilled and terrified her. Priya's breath quickened as she clung to the little comfort they shared, yet the fear of losing it all painted her thoughts in shades of gray. She imagined Rohan's face, the kindness in his gaze, a stark reminder of everything she stood to lose. But with Zayed, there was a possibility—one she had never dared to hope for before.

As the call ended, both found themselves drenched in silence. Priya's heart thundered against her ribcage as she stared at the blank screen, the weight of a decision crashing down upon her. Could they navigate through this labyrinth of emotion and obligation? The deepening connection twisted like a vine around her heart, and even if she yearned for the warmth of his embrace, the road stretched ahead was fraught with peril.

Unexpected Conversations

Days turned into weeks, and the distance between Priya and Zayed transformed from a physical void into a twisted tapestry of words that stitched their hearts together. Each message sent through whispers of technology bore the weight of their unexpressed feelings; the careful selection of words often concealed more than it revealed. It was this distance that allowed them to explore parts of themselves they had long buried under layers of duty.

During one of their late-night conversations, Zayed shared a personal story about his childhood in Qatar, the endless summers filled with the warmth of familial gatherings. Priya listened intently, her heart beating with a mix of admiration and longing. She found herself enchanted by the vivid imagery he painted with his words, yearning not only for a connection with him but also for the life he seemed to embody –

one filled with laughter, joy, and the love of family. In that moment, she felt the weight of her own loneliness swell, amplifying an ache she thought she had buried beneath her responsibilities.

"I used to play in the gardens of my grandfather's estate," Zayed said, his voice a low rumble through the phone. "He would tell me stories of the stars, how each one had a soul, a story, just like us. I always believed there was magic in those tales."

His words lingered in the air like the remnants of a dream, pulling her into a world where possibilities danced just out of reach.

Risk of Discovery

The distance that separated Priya and Zayed felt both agonizing and exhilarating as they navigated their secret communication. Each text, each late-night video call, became a fragile lifeline, binding their hearts despite the miles and the expectations tying them to their respective lives. Priya often found herself perched on the edge of her bed, her heart racing as she awaited Zayed's messages, her fingers hovering over the screen like a moth drawn to a flame.

Yet with every interaction, the thrill of their clandestine connection was marred by a shadow of anxiety. Both of them played a delicate game, weaving through their realities, the stakes growing higher with each passing day. What had begun as innocent curiosity had spiraled into an emotional tempest, and every sweet word spoken over the screen echoed with the dire consequences they could not ignore—what if they were discovered?

Priya lay awake one night, staring at the ceiling, the weight of her secret pressing down on her chest like a boulder. Shadows danced on the walls, conjuring images of Rohan's warm smile, his quiet support that now felt like a shackle. How could she betray his trust? And what of Zayed? He was trapped in a different web of expectations, yet his longing resonated deeply within her. Each secret look, each shared smile across crowded rooms filled with laughter and discussions masked the turbulence brewing beneath the surface. Priya's heart clenched at the thought of her life unraveling. The intersections of their hearts and the threat of discovery started to feel like a ticking clock, counting down to an inevitable finale.

One evening, under the guise of a typical workday filled with bustling patients and endless tasks, Priya received a notification that sent a chill straight through her. It was a message from Zayed, tinged with urgency, urging her to meet. They had strayed into treacherous territory, and even now, the thought of meeting filled her with a potent mix of excitement and dread. "What if our spouses find out?" The fear of exposure hovered over her like a dark cloud, overshadowing every glimmer of hope that they could navigate the complexity of their growing feelings. Yet, the temptation to see him—to feel the warmth of his presence, to taste the sweetness of their shared laughter—was nearly irresistible.

In the days leading to the rendezvous, Priya was a bundle of nerves, her heart pounding as she carefully planned every detail. The anticipated meeting was like a siren's call, as exhilarating as it was perilous. Underneath the anxious flutter lay the crushing reality: every stolen moment bore the potential for ruin. She looked at her reflection, the woman she saw staring back was a blend of longing and guilt, the struggle of her dual existence etched in her eyes. What would happen if she were spotted with Zayed? Would it simply be a breath of misfortune, or would it lead to a catastrophic revelation that would shatter their worlds?

Yet, something deep within her craved that touch of danger. The thrill of the unknown danced tantalizingly close, yet echoed with the haunting inference of consequences. As the hour of their meeting drew closer, Priya's heart raced with an intoxicating mixture of trepidation and longing. As she slipped into her dress—a bold crimson that showcased her inner fire—she felt a resolve bubble beneath her uncertainty. Perhaps they could find a way to navigate their tumultuous sea of emotions without capsizing their lives. But even as she clung to this glimmer of hope, a warning whispered in the back of her mind: sometimes, the greatest risks yield the most devastating discoveries.

13
Seeds of Doubt

Growing Suspicion from Spouses

Days turned into weeks following the conference, and although Priya and Zayed maintained a semblance of normalcy in their respective lives, an undeniable tension now hung thick in the air. Rohan, with his gentle but increasingly watchful eyes, began to sense the subtle shifts in Priya. The fleeting smiles on her lips lingered a bit too long after a phone call, and her late-night work sessions became suspiciously frequent.

Meanwhile, in Doha, Sheikha Fatima felt the weight of her husband's newfound distance. Zayed, usually attentive and engaging, now carried a shadow in his gaze. Their conversations felt like a performance, staccato and forced, lacking the warmth that had once characterized their bond. Fatima, a perceptive woman, noted the slight changes in his demeanor—a lingering gaze at his phone, a half-hearted smile at dinner that didn't quite reach his eyes.

Sensations of doubt gnawed at both Rohan and Fatima as they individually began to piece together the unspoken clues. A forgotten text message, a call ended too abruptly, an email left open with a name that ignited curiosity. The air was charged with unuttered questions and veiled observations. Priya found herself walking a tightrope, balancing her sworn commitments to her husband and the magnetic pull toward Zayed. The heart wants what it wants, and yet both she and Zayed remained acutely aware of the stakes at play.

The first real crack in their façades emerged during a dinner at Rohan and Priya's home. Rohan, keenly observant, asked Priya about an unfamiliar name he had overheard during a call: Zayed. The name dropped heavily between them, like a stone plunging into water, sending ripples of unease across Priya's heart. Her mind raced, desperately seeking a diversion, a place to hide her mounting anxiety.

Likewise, Fatima arranged for a dinner with Zayed where she projected confidence, but inside, she was reeling. As they sat across from each other, the clinking of dishes contrasted sharply with the silence of their thoughts.

"Are you happy, Zayed?" she asked abruptly, her voice trembling slightly.

He hesitated, wrestling with the ambiguity of his feelings. The truth loomed close, testing the delicate fabric of their marriage, threatening to unravel into chaos.

Outside, the stars twinkled brightly, oblivious to the turmoil igniting in the hearts of both couples. As Priya and Zayed carried on, tethered by their secret but edged closer to the precipice of discovery, the tension multiplied. Would they confront the shadows lurking in their spouses' hearts? Or would the unspoken truths forever haunt them in silence?

Unintentional Revelations

As Priya sat in the bustling café, her thoughts spiraled around the whirlwind of emotions she had navigated since meeting Zayed. Each day felt like an emotional tug of war, with her heart latching onto memories of their shared moments, while her mind echoed the weight of her commitments back home. The warm sunlight streamed through the windows, dancing on the surface of her coffee, but within her, uncertainty brewed like a storm.

Back in Qatar, Zayed felt the tension rising in his household. Sheikha Fatima had become unusually observant, her perceptive nature sharpened by what she couldn't yet articulate. As she served dinner, Fatima's gaze flickered over her husband with a sharpness that made Zayed's heart race for all the wrong reasons. Each silence felt loaded, each word twisted in ways that made familiarity feel foreign.

Just a casual conversation with their friends took on new weight when they discussed professional commitments, and both tried to mask their discomfort.

"Zayed's been so busy lately... I wonder where he's finding the time?" Fatima vented, half-hearted laughter concealing her true feelings.

Each shared glance, laden with veiled implications, sent ripples of doubt through Zayed. He wondered if the walls he'd built around his heart would truly protect him from the storm brewing in their midst.

In Mumbai, Rohan had noticed Priya's sporadic distractions, her faraway looks eliciting a knot of unease in his stomach. He was aware that their life together, while secure, had become devoid of sparks. A missed text here, a late return from work there—everything seemed to amplify the gap unspoken between them. And yet, every time he reached for her, he was met with cold indifference, a chasm that seemed only to widen with time.

One evening, as she prepped for her medical presentation, Priya's phone buzzed with a message from Zayed—a gentle reminder of their shared dreams, a soft declaration of support. It was the kind of acknowledgment that made her heart leap, but the thrill was quickly quenched by the realization of her responsibilities. Disturbed, she placed the phone face down, but the seeds of doubt began to germinate fiercely in both households.

Rohan, growing increasingly suspicious, decided to confront Priya one evening after an uncomfortable silence settled between them.

"Is there someone else?" he asked, the question edged with a vulnerability he'd hidden all too well.

Priya turned, startled, and felt the room tilt on its axis. The underlying guilt crashed over her like a tidal wave, and she struggled to keep her voice steady.

At that same moment, Zayed sat across from Fatima during dinner, drowning in an unfamiliar guilt at the table. Fatima's question hung in the air like a stormcloud:

"You've changed, Zayed. What is going on with you?"

There was no easy way to answer, no way to give a name to the unnameable feelings coursing through him. With every beat of his heart, the territory he had wandered into felt less and less like home.

As evening deepened into night, both couples felt the specter of doubt closing in. What had once been threads of connection began to fray, unraveling the fabric of trust. Priya and Zayed's silence spoke volumes, each caught in the web of unintentional revelations that spiraled beyond their control. And the truth? It was lurking just beneath the surface, waiting for a moment to pounce, to illuminate the dark corners of their lives.

Unbeknownst to them, whispers of suspicion danced through the air, curling around them with an insidious grace. On either side of the ocean, hearts beat in rhythm, straddling the line between cinematic romance and the harsh reality of betrayal, threatening to expose the fracture lines that had been drawn in the shadows. Only time would reveal whether love would triumph over the heavy burden of their choices or if they would all succumb to the inevitable erosion of trust.

Navigating Tense Interactions

The air was thick with tension as Rohan and Zayed found themselves in the same lavishly appointed lounge at the conference in Dubai. Rohan, aware of the shifts in Priya's demeanor over the past weeks, felt the gnawing claws of insecurity as he turned to Zayed, who effortlessly dominated the room with a charming smile. Though Rohan recognized Zayed's status and success, his jealousy bubbled just beneath the surface, a haze clouded by his growing suspicions.

Zayed greeted Rohan with a courteous nod, his gaze flicking toward the vast city skyline visible through the floor-to-ceiling windows. He could sense Rohan's discomfort, an electricity crackling in the air, yet he held a mask of composure, mastering the art of diplomacy. Beneath that facade, however, Zayed shared in Rohan's unacknowledged dread—the bond he had with Priya might ignite a precarious spark of conflict between them.

"Congratulations on your esteemed work," Rohan began, his voice steady but laced with an undercurrent of challenge, "I must say, it's impressive how influential your foundation has become."

There was no mistaking the intent behind his words; Rohan was weighing each syllable, measuring his rival's reaction. Zayed merely acknowledged the compliment with a polite smile, feeling the tension weave tighter like a noose around them.

"And your wife's dedication to her patients is commendable," Zayed replied, injecting a layer of sincerity into his tone, though he felt the weight of Rohan's gaze sharpening.

The official praise felt hollow to him, knowing the emotional distance shrouding Priya's heart. He hadn't imagined the ripples of their connection would disrupt the calm surface of anyone else's life, least of all Rohan's.

As they exchanged pleasantries, the room around them faded into a mere backdrop for their standoff. Rohan's posture betrayed his anxiety; he stood rigid, fingers tense against the edge of the bar, a façade of control masking a tempest of fear. Zayed, on the other hand, appeared relaxed outwardly but was keenly aware of the precarious nature of their connection—a dance on a tightrope, perilous yet intoxicating.

Then came a shared glance—an almost imperceptible moment where their eyes locked, curiosity mingled with suspicion, and the world around them narrowed to a singular urgency. Rohan's heart raced as the realization struck: he had to confront the truth, to peel back the layers of this insidious doubt that had crept into his marriage.

"I've always admired your dedication to philanthropy, Zayed," he said, his voice dropping almost conspiratorially, "but one must wonder, how far does that dedication extend?"

The inquiry hung between them like a pendulum, echoing in the silence. A fleeting moment passed, and Zayed felt the pressure of the challenge surge. The gesture, though subtle, was palpable—a challenge, a quest for transparency amidst the shadows. Rohan was probing, seeking assurance that there was no intermingling of their lives beyond the professional realm, yet he could not shake the feeling that probing deeper might shatter their tenuous alliance.

"I strive to make a difference wherever I can," Zayed answered, veiling the deeper truths that lingered close to his heart. He sensed the unspoken accusation within Rohan's question: Did his philanthropic endeavors overshadow personal commitments? As they stood on the precipice of honesty, the tension thickened, and Zayed recognized that the navigation between personal and professional bonds had become treacherous territory.

As the two men measured each other, Priya remained oblivious to the high-stakes encounter unfolding just across the lounge. Somewhere between her memories of shared dreams and the vibrant pulse of the city outside, she felt the weight of their decisions shifting. Still, love knotted with responsibilities, and uncertainty lurked in the corners of every interaction.

"Are we not bound by our commitments?" Rohan's voice cut through Zayed's contemplative haze, piercing with an underlying menace.

The question lingered in the air as Rohan's eyes mingled fury with fear, igniting a storm that would challenge the foundational structures of both their lives. Zayed's breath hitched; the calm facade he had constructed began to creak under Rohan's scrutiny, the threat of exposure looming large.

"Commitments," Zayed echoed softly, recognizing that the very notion could either bind or free them.

The hesitation was agonizing, yet it underscored their complex realities threaded together by unspoken feelings—a dazzling enigma that could unravel everything they had built, both personally and professionally. That awareness hung between them like an unsung tune, reaching a crescendo they both feared would spill over into the open.

As the evening wore on, the friction between them transformed into an electrifying charge. They both felt it—a shift, the gravity of a choice that could lead to ruin or redemption. The stakes had been raised, the game transformed from professional courtesy to intense scrutiny, and in that lounge, paths began to diverge ominously, setting the stage for the chaos that lay ahead.

14
Truths Unraveled

Confrontation and Accusations

As dusk settled over the city, an unsettling tension filled the air at Zayed's elegant penthouse, a stark contrast to the opulence surrounding them. Priya and Zayed stood in the living room, shadows of their unspoken feelings cast against the grand windows overlooking the shimmering skyline of Doha. Their hearts raced with the weight of secrets and the risk of their newfound emotional entanglement. Just moments before, laughter had echoed through the walls; now, their silence spoke volumes.

Suddenly, the door swung open. Sheikha Fatima stormed in, her stride purposeful and her eyes ablaze with fury. Instantly, the warmth of the room evaporated, replaced with icy tension.

"I've just spoken to Rohan," she declared, her voice sharp and unyielding. "And he's been asking questions. Questions I do not have answers to."

Priya felt as if the ground beneath her had shifted; the sense of safety she had known wavered as the air thickened with accusations. Zayed's features hardened as he stood between the two women, caught in an emotional crossfire.

"What does he know?" Zayed asked, his voice steady but laced with a hint of panic.

Priya felt her breath catch; every ounce of her body wanted to be assured, to believe that their impromptu meetings would not lead to this moment. Fatima's stare pierced through Priya, leaving her feeling exposed and vulnerable.

"He knows something is amiss. I've noticed changes in him, and you," she pointed at Priya, "there's something different about you."

Priya's heart raced. She had wanted to be strong, but here, confronted by the truth, her resolve began to crumble.

"This is not what it seems," Zayed spoke, trying to reclaim control of the situation.

Priya could see the desperation in his

eyes, a silent plea for unity against the storm brewing. But how could she stand firm when the very foundation of their connection felt like a house of cards? Fatima's response dripped with incredulity:

"Not what it seems? I think it's exactly what it seems! Are you two trying to unravel everything we've built?"

The weight of societal expectations bore down on them, creating a palpable rift.

As the confrontation continued, accusations spiraled, intertwining personal insecurities with cultural pressures.

"You're a physician, Priya! How can you betray your marriage?"

Fatima's tone softened momentarily, revealing a hint of pain beneath her anger.

Priya felt suffocated by the reality of her choices, aware that her desire for fulfillment had come at an unimaginable cost.

"I didn't intend for this to happen," Priya finally managed, her voice shaking, "but Zayed... he understands me in ways I never thought possible."

The air crackled with tension as both women stood resolute, each entwined in their pain yet fiercely protective of their respective families. Zayed moved closer to Fatima, desperation etched across his handsome face.

"Please, let's talk about this rationally—" he began, but the intensity of emotions brewed like a storm ready to break. He had never seen Fatima so agitated, her steadfast demeanor fracturing under the strain of uncovered betrayals.

"Rationality?" Fatima scoffed, "Do you really think we can solve this with reason? You've put everything we are at risk! How can I trust you now, Zayed?"

His heart sank. The delicate threads of trust began to unravel, exposing raw emotions and looming decisions. All the while, Priya stood at the center, feeling the life she had known slipping further from her grasp. The confrontation grew increasingly chaotic, a whirlpool of accusations and insecurities swirling around them, with Priya caught between her love for Zayed and her loyalty to Rohan. The truth behind the secret they had shared now became a destructive force, threatening to obliterate their lives.

With each harsh word and furious glance, Priya felt the foundations of her world starting to crack. Hidden in the shadows of their lives, societal expectations began to surface, intertwining with emotions they had never fully understood. The confrontation had finally brought their truth to light, forged not by love but complicated by duty, betrayal, and longing. And as voices escalated and tears glistened, Priya knew that nothing could ever be the same again.

Societal Pressures Mounting

As Priya and Zayed stood on the precipice of their intertwined lives, the weight of societal expectations loomed heavily over them, threatening to dismantle the fragile connection they had built. The vibrant atmosphere of the conference hall in Dubai felt suffocating, each laughter and whisper echoing the judgment that awaited them outside. Priya's heart raced as she thought of Rohan, the gentle kindness he embodied, and the life they had built together. Yet, the magnetic pull of Zayed's presence constantly tugged at her conscience, demanding her attention where she dared not let it tread.

Zayed, too, felt the oppressive gaze of tradition bearing down upon him. In the luxurious world of Qatari elites, infidelity carried not only personal shame but a stark societal condemnation that he had been raised to fear. Every interaction with Priya felt like a step towards forbidden territory, and yet, the allure of their shared dreams and illuminated aspirations cast a powerful spell over his resolve. Would the public scrutiny and familial pressures crush his desire for a deeper connection? The juxtaposition of his opulent lifestyle against the backdrop of love unexpressed felt like living a double life, one that he never anticipated navigating.

With the end of the conference approaching, Priya and Zayed's secret glances exchanged across crowded rooms turned into hurried conversations, fraught with the weight of all that remained unspoken. Each passing moment deepened the emotional stakes, blending excitement with an impending dread they could no longer ignore. The looming threats of exposure tightened their senses; every smile from Rohan and friendly nod from Sheikha Fatima seared into their minds as unwelcome reminders of their haunting reality. They were no longer just lovers caught in a web of passion; they were two hearts navigating a labyrinth of social expectations and familial bonds that threatened to ensnare them at every turn.

As they prepared for one last evening together, the tension among the conference attendees grew palpable, whispers of speculation beginning to swirl. With Zayed's high-profile status, any flicker of scandal would ignite like wildfire, reaching far beyond the privilege of their private worlds. Priya felt a momentary flicker of panic as they exchanged their final looks, as if they both knew these moments were numbered. The intersection of love and dread at that moment felt almost poetic, yet terrifying. Their hearts raced in tandem, aware that the societal pressures they both faced were not just the limitations of their respective cultures, but an imminent threat that could unravel everything. Would this be a night of liberation or the beginning of their undoing?

In the throes of darkness that enveloped them, they both faced a choice that loomed larger than the mere act of affection. As they moved closer, the world around them blurred, and each beat of their hearts echoed the imminent truth: to embrace love was to potentially ignite a storm that neither could control. What if the buzz of the conference could turn lethal, transforming from a moment of intimacy into a cacophony of accusations? How long could they continue this dance before one misstep led to the exposure of their forbidden desires? There, in that heated moment beneath the fluorescent lights and amidst the fleeting laughter, they could barely breathe as the palpable weight of familial and societal expectations bore down upon them, threatening to shatter the very fabric of their lives.

Shattered Trust

The air was thick with tension as Priya stood at the threshold of her own turmoil, having just emerged from a confrontation with Rohan that had revealed her deepest fears. The words hung heavy in the space between them, where love had once flourished but now was marred by a gnawing betrayal. She could feel Rohan's eyes drilling into her, brimming with hurt and confusion, the once gentle gaze now sharp and accusatory.

Zayed, meanwhile, faced a similar cataclysm in his own home. Sheikha Fatima's voice echoed in his mind, her questions cutting through the silence like a dagger. With each inquiry about his late nights, his distant demeanor, and his waning enthusiasm for their life, Zayed felt the walls of his carefully constructed world start to crumble. He had long been the man of tradition and duty, yet the thrill of his connection with Priya had awakened something profound—something Fatima could never understand.

As Priya paced their living room, a pervading sense of dread overcame her. She thought of Zayed and their impossible connection that had ignited a fire in her heart, a flame that felt both dangerous and intoxicating. But the weight of Rohan's anguish forced her to reevaluate everything. The mention of divorce floated in the air, a phantom that laughed at her despair, daring her to abandon her responsibilities. With every hour they spent apart, her heart ached, the longing for Zayed intensifying as the reality of her marriage bore down like a vice grip.

Unbeknownst to her, Zayed was wrestling with the same demons. He was trapped in a dialogue with Fatima that twisted like a knife in his gut, each accusation leading him toward the precipice of confession. What was a man to do when the heart's desires clashed with the weight of familial expectations? He felt a gravity pulling him toward Priya, yet here he was, struggling to keep his footing in a world rich with obligations. Would he dare to shatter the trust he had built with his family for a love that seemed destined for heartbreak?

As Priya and Zayed faced their spouses in fervent exchanges, the true stakes became evident: hearts hanging by a thread, marriages teetering on the brink. The looming specter of societal judgment added to their internal strife, leaving them to ponder the choices that led them here and what it would mean to unravel the fabric of their lives altogether. Outside, the world continued its relentless march forward, unaware of the storm brewing within the walls of two homes, two hearts aflame with both desire and fear.

With each confrontation came revelations, punctuated by harsh truths and veiled accusations. Priya felt the ground beneath her feet unstable, while Zayed realized that the pillars of tradition he had

held sacred could either protect him or imprison him. As the emotional undercurrents
surged, the thought of losing Priya clawed
at his sanity, igniting an urgency within him
to act, to choose.

Time seemed to stretch, and Priya found
herself standing at a crossroads proph-
esized by anguish—the relentless pull of
love against the immutable chains of duty.
Desperation clawed at her throat, making
breathing difficult, and she found herself
asking the question that threatened to shatter everything: How far could she go to reclaim herself?

Zayed, too, was poised at the edge of an
abyss, grappling with a decision that could
alter his life forever. Would he choose the
safety of his family or risk it all for a love that
promised freedom? Only fate could judge
the final course, but the cracks were already
beginning to show, and the question remained: Was trust merely an illusion, waiting for the moment to be shattered?

15
The Endless Decision

Reflections on Love and Duty

Priya stood on the balcony of her apartment in Mumbai, the city lights twinkling like distant stars against the night sky. The hustle and bustle that defined her life faded into a quiet hum as she wrestled with the gravity of her emotions. Love was supposed to be a sanctuary, a refuge from the demands of duty, yet she found herself ensnared in a web of obligations that felt suffocating. Every heartbeat echoed the unresolved tension of a love that felt both exhilarating and forbidden.

With Zayed's image etched in her mind, she pondered the stark contrast of their worlds. He was a man of immense privilege, guided by family legacies and societal expectations, yet beneath his affluent exterior was a yearning for authenticity. Their shared moments, filled with laughter and whispered secrets, felt imbued with a warmth she had long thought extinguished in her own life. Her marriage to Rohan, marked by mutual respect but lacking in passion, made her question the choices that had defined her.

The phone buzzed, pulling her from her thoughts. It was Zayed.

"I've been thinking about you," he texted, his words igniting a familiar surge of emotion. She felt a thrill run down her spine—a mixture of excitement and guilt. Each conversation with him was both a balm and a burden; it elevated her spirit while also dragging her deeper into a chasm of conflicting responsibilities. Would their love conquer their duties, or would it become another casualty of the life they had settled for?

As the night deepened, Priya wrestled with her choices. What would it mean to follow her heart? To seek the connection and passion she yearned for? A part of her was desperate to run away, to step into a future with Zayed where love wasn't tainted by duty. But reality was a fierce opponent;

her dreams collided with the responsibilities she had to Rohan, to her family, to her patients.

Unbeknownst to her, Zayed was lost in similar reflections, standing in his penthouse in Doha, looking out over the vast expanse of the desert. The grandeur of his surroundings felt hollow compared to the thrill Priya sparked within him. Their whispered confessions in the quiet corners of the conference seemed to resonate with every fiber of his being. Yet, as he turned his gaze to the moonlit horizon, he knew he was caught between two worlds—the love that bloomed like a forbidden orchard and the family legacy that demanded his loyalty.

Both Priya and Zayed were at a crossroads, each heart clinging to the fragile thread of their connection while weighed down by the heavy mantle of duty. A silent, unspoken tension stretched between them, one filled with anticipation and fear. What awaited them if they took the plunge? Would violating the walls of their married lives break them apart or bind them closer together? The answers felt impossibly far away as they each held on to the desperate hope that love could transcend the boundaries of their realities.

As Priya's thoughts turned darker, the flutter of her heart morphed into a storm of uncertainties. She picked up her phone once more, trembling fingers hovering over Zayed's name. Should she reach out? Now, at this precise moment, facing the weight of her decision, the fear of discovery loomed on the horizon like a tempest ready to break. It was a moment to choose—love or duty, desire or obligation. And in the silence that stretched between them, both were poised on the brink of an irrevocable choice that would shape their futures.

The Final Standoff

The air between Priya and Zayed crackled with tension as they stood in the dimly lit conference room, the weight of their choices pressing down like an invisible leaden cloak. Each blink felt like a countdown, a silent acknowledgment of the inevitable confrontation that loomed ahead. The stark white walls around them seemed to lean in, amplifying the shattering silence as they exchanged glances filled with unspoken questions and hidden desires.

Priya's heart raced, filled with the remnants of shared secrets only they understood. Memories of laughter tinged with longing flooded her mind—the fleeting moments that had stitched their lives together despite the vast chasm of tradition and expectation that separated them. She could hardly breathe, caught in the throes of an emotional tempest, teetering precariously between love and duty. What did it mean to love someone fiercely while tethered to another life, filled with obligations and a partner she respected but did not quite love?

Zayed's steady gaze was a storm of his own, filled with silent conflict. The world outside continued on, but here, inside this room, they existed on the precipice of a decision that would alter the course of their lives forever. He wanted to reach out, to bridge the gap between their realities, yet the heavy reminders of his family's expectations loomed large. Sheikha Fatima and the life he had built stood like daunting sentinels, ready to pounce at the first sign of weakness. Yet, within himself, Zayed felt the fierce urge to shatter those chains, to pursue something authentic, however daring it may be.

"Priya," Zayed began, his voice barely more than a whisper, laden with the gravity of their situation. "We can't keep doing this. It's tearing me apart."

His words hung in the air, thick and heavy, as if he had drawn a boundary line in the sands of their shared reality. Each syllable was a plea wrapped in desperation, fighting against the myriad responsibilities that anchored him in place.

She felt her heart clench at his words, fear and longing waging war within her.

"I know," she replied quietly, feeling the truth of her own words slice through her own pretense. "But what choice do we have? Our lives are tangled in ways I didn't anticipate."

The confession bared her soul, the vulnerability swallowing her whole as tears threatened to spill. If only they could find a way to disentangle their fates from the expectations that suffocated them.

Yet, with every second that passed, the reality of their situation settled upon them like frost on autumn leaves—beautiful yet excruciatingly cold. No one had prepared them for the stakes they had raised, for the exquisite pain of loving while shackled to another. Time stretched thin, teetering on the edge of creation and destruction.

Then, without warning, the tenuous fabric of their secret world ripped apart when the door swung open, revealing Rohan's silhouette. His expression clouded with confusion and suspicion, the air turned dense with unspoken truths.

"Priya? What's going on here?"

His voice cracked like thunder, echoing through the room, sending shivers down Priya's spine. The world, once so filled with possibilities, narrowed down into a singular moment of dread.

In that instant, the weight of their choices hung starkly in the air; they could no longer hide behind their carefully constructed façades. Priya's heart raced as she faced Rohan, taken from the comfort of routine into the jagged edges of revelation. The choices they had tried to avoid, the emotions they had tried to tame, surged forth, entwining with the chaos resonating from Zayed's stillness, and Priya realized the path forward would no longer be navigated in silence.

The confrontation was imminent; a trial of heart and mind that would demand sacrifices as the true nature of their feelings emerged, thrusting them painfully closer to decisions that could shatter everything they knew. Time trembled at the brink of an irreversible change, leaving Priya and Zayed to grapple with the reality that love, while a beautiful sanctuary, could also serve as a tempest, destructive in its fury.

A New Path Forward

Priya stood at the precipice of her life, her heart racing against the backdrop of the vast, starry sky that spread above her like a tapestry woven from the fabric of her dreams and fears. She had never anticipated that a fleeting connection with Zayed, a man from a world so different from hers, would throw her entire being into turmoil. Yet here she was, teetering between the comfort of the known and the exhilarating yet terrifying unknown. The weight of her responsibilities and the warmth of her husband's familiarity juxtaposed sharply against the electric pull towards Zayed.

As she recalled their stolen moments together, the laughter they shared, and the deep conversations that revealed her soul like never before, confusion swept over her. How could something that felt so right be so wrong? The walls of her arranged marriage loomed around her, constructed with duty and expectation, yet the foundations had begun to crack under the pressure of her longing. With Zayed, she had glimpsed a life of passion, of fulfillment beyond medical charts and hospital corridors. But could she truly abandon everything she had ever known for a whim of the heart?

Meanwhile, on another continent, Zayed paced the opulent halls of his family estate, where the weight of legacy tugged at his very core. His arranged life with Sheikha Fatima was like a gilded cage, beautiful yet suffocating. The joy of fatherhood brought him immense pride, yet he often found himself staring out at the horizon, yearning for something—or someone—he could not quite grasp. Every moment spent with Priya had seeded a different kind of hope, one that promised a world where love was not a transaction but an intoxicating adventure. Could he dare to break free and carve out a new path that embraced both love and obligation?

Both of them, connected yet worlds apart,

began to understand that their lives had converged at a crucial junction. The boundaries they had previously accepted were now frail and shaky. Fate had unpinned their lives from the ordinary, and their souls craved a reckoning. As the reality of their situations bore down upon them, the stakes became alarmingly clear. To pursue this connection meant risking lives meticulously built and hearts meticulously guarded. Each day that passed brought new opportunities, but also the looming question: could they both confront the societal expectations that dictated their lives, or would they forever remain prisoners of their circumstances?

The clock was ticking, and every passing minute added layers of tension to their respective lives. Echoes of past decisions lingered, reminding them of all they had to lose, yet the allure of something more profound urged them forward. In this fragile space, where dreams met reality, Priya and Zayed found themselves swept away by the tides of possibility. If life offered a new path forward, would they gather the courage to take the first step?

The End.